FAIRY
CHARM

A charm bracelet opens
a magical world of adventure

D0589738

FAIRY CHARM

A charm bracelet opens
a magical world of adventure

The Star Cloak
The Peskie Spell
The Rainbow Wand

EMILY RODDA

Catnip
PUBLISHING LTD

The Fairy Charm series
by Emily Rodda

The Charm Bracelet
The Flower Fairies
The Third Wish
The Last Fairy-Apple Tree
The Magic Key
The Unicorn
The Star Cloak
The Water Sprites
The Peskie Spell
The Rainbow Wand

CATNIP BOOKS
Published by Catnip Publishing Ltd.
14 Greville Street
London EC1N 8SB

This edition published 2008
1 3 5 7 9 10 8 6 4 2

First published by the Australian Broadcasting Corporation,
GPO Box 9994 Sydney, NSW 2001

Text copyright © Emily Rodda, 2000

ISBN 978-1-84647-045-5

Printed in Poland

www.catnippublishing.co.uk

Contents

The Star Cloak

The Peskie Spell

The Rainbow Wand

FAIRY CHARM

A charm bracelet opens
a magical world of adventure

The Star Cloak

EMILY RODDA

CHAPTER ONE

Starry Night

essie turned over in bed and looked at the clock on her bedside table. It was nearly midnight, but sleep was as far away as ever. She was tingling with excitement, just as she'd been ever since the first star appeared in the sky above the old house called Blue Moon.

The night sky always looked brighter in the mountains, away from the city lights. But never had Jessie seen it as it was tonight. Tonight, the moon was almost full, and the stars were *blazing*. Just looking at them made Jessie quiver.

'I don't feel sleepy at all,' she'd said to her grandmother soon after her mother had left for night duty at the hospital. 'It's really weird. I feel all excited—as if something wonderful is going to happen.'

Granny had raised her eyebrows in surprise. 'Of course, Jessie,' she'd said. 'How else would you feel the night before—?' Then she'd broken off, shaking her head. 'Oh, how silly of me!' she'd exclaimed. 'I was thinking you knew all about it, but of course you don't! This time a year ago you and Rosemary were clearing out your house in the city, ready to move here. You missed last Wish Night.'

'*Wish Night?*' Jessie had said, her eyes widening with excitement. 'You mean . . . like in Grandpa's painting?'

'Oh, yes,' Granny had said. 'Tomorrow night, a few minutes after the first star appears, Wish Night will begin in the Realm. The stars are getting ready for it there, and even here, in the mortal world, they seem to come closer. Even here, there's magic in the air. I feel it—and so do you.'

Jessie had hugged herself with excitement. No wonder she felt as if something wonderful was about to happen. It was!

'Do you think I could go to the Realm tomorrow night?' she'd asked breathlessly. 'Could I be there for Wish Night?'

Granny had laughed. 'I don't see why not,' she'd said, her green eyes twinkling. 'In fact, I'm sure your friends are expecting you to come on the most exciting night of the Realm year. All the more reason for you to get to bed now, Jessie. It's getting late, and you might have trouble falling asleep. I always do, just before Wish Night.'

Wish Night.

Jessie turned over in bed again, her heart fluttering as she thought of the beautiful picture that hung in the Blue Moon hallway, just near the front door. Her grandfather, Robert Belairs, had painted that picture. It was one of his most famous fairyland paintings and had been photographed for many books.

It showed a huge crowd of fairy folk and magical creatures gathered in front of a golden palace. A beautiful woman with flowing red hair, wearing a silver crown and a glittering pale blue cloak, was standing on the top of the palace steps, her arms raised. Everyone was looking up at the night sky, which was filled with falling stars that lit the darkness with flashing trails of silver light and filled the air with sparkling magic.

People visiting Blue Moon for the first time almost always stopped and looked at the painting.

When at last they turned away from it they were always smiling, as if it had filled them with good feelings.

'It's called "Wish Night",' Granny would say when they told her how much they liked the painting. 'You know that you can make a wish if you see a falling star, don't you? Well, imagine a night when the whole sky is full of them!'

Then the visitors would sigh and say what a wonderful imagination Robert Belairs must have had to think of something like that, then paint it so that it seemed so real.

Little did they know, Jessie thought, that her grandfather had painted something he'd actually seen. Little did they know that behind a hedge at the bottom of the Blue Moon garden was an invisible Door that led to the fairy world of the Realm, and that Robert Belairs had visited the Realm many, many times.

And none of them dreamed that old, white-haired Jessica Belairs, with her bright green eyes and sweet smile, was the daughter of that beautiful red-haired fairy queen in the painting. They didn't dream that more than fifty years ago a princess born to be the Realm's true queen had fallen in love with Robert Belairs and left her own world to marry him, leaving her younger sister Helena to rule in her place. That was Granny's secret—the secret only Jessie shared.

This time last year I'd only just discovered the Realm, Jessie thought. It all still seemed like a wonderful dream. Sometimes it still does!

But the Realm was no dream: the golden charm bracelet lying on Jessie's bedside table was proof of that. Every charm that hung from the bracelet had been a gift from the Realm. Every one held wonderful memories of the adventures Jessie had shared with her Realm friends: Maybelle the miniature horse, Giff the elf, and Patrice the palace housekeeper. Whenever she touched the bracelet, her mind filled with pictures of fairies, pixies, gnomes, griffins, mermaids, unicorns, Queen Helena, and the beautiful people called the Folk.

Tomorrow night I'll see Wish Night for myself, Jessie thought. I'll see the sky of the Realm filled with falling stars, just like in Grandpa's painting. And I'll be able to make a wish!

She gazed longingly at the window. There was nothing she wanted more than to pull the curtains open and look at the stars one more time.

Stop this, she told herself firmly. You've got to

get some sleep. Tomorrow's a school day. If you look half-asleep in class, Ms Stone will say you're daydreaming again and keep you in at lunchtime for another one of her 'little talks'.

She frowned, thinking of Ms Stone's cool, calm voice and pale blue eyes, of Ms Stone's smooth, fair hair drawn so tightly back from her face that her skin seemed stretched. What a contrast to their old teacher, Ms Hewson!

Ms Hewson had untidy, curly brown hair and glasses that were always slipping down her freckled nose. When she laughed, or was cross, her face went bright red. Her class was sometimes noisy, but it had always been fun—or almost always. Things were very different now.

Oh, why did Ms Hewson have to go off and have a baby! Jessie thought irritably. I *liked* Ms Hewson. Everyone liked her. But Ms Stone . . .

Ms Stone wasn't a teacher anyone could actually *like*. She was young and very good-looking. Her elegant clothes always looked as if they'd just come back from the cleaners. She never raised her voice. She was well organised, calm and logical.

But she was just *too* calm, *too* logical. It was as if she had no more feelings than a computer. She never lost her temper, but she never laughed, either. She smiled sometimes, of course, but the smile stayed at her mouth and never reached her eyes.

She also despised anything she saw as fanciful or silly or not part of the real world. This was why she hadn't chosen Jessie's story to be a finalist in the Spring Fair children's writing competition, which this year was being judged by Petra Connelly, a very well-known children's writer.

'You really must learn to use your talent more wisely, Jessica,' Ms Stone had said in her calm, cool voice. 'Your little story was quite well written, but the subject—gnomes and unicorns and so on— was completely unsuitable for your age group. By now you should be writing about real people, real problems—things that matter.'

My stories are about things that matter, Jessie thought fiercely. At least they matter to me! And Ms Hewson always liked them a lot. Why shouldn't Petra Connelly like them, too?

This was no way to get to sleep. Jessie pushed the memory of Ms Stone's voice out of her mind. She turned over again, snuggled deep under her warm quilt, and tried to think happy, peaceful thoughts.

She thought about how she loved Blue Moon,

and how glad she was that she and her mother had moved from the city to live with Granny. She thought about her friend Sal, who had told her not to let old Stone-face get her down. She thought about the Realm. . . .

The old clock in the living room began to strike midnight. Dreamily, Jessie counted the chimes.

. . . nine, ten, eleven, twelve . . .

And as the last chime died away, she heard something else—something that made her sit bolt upright. Someone was tapping at her window. And there was a voice, whispering urgently.

'Jessie! Jessie!'

CHAPTER TWO

Problems

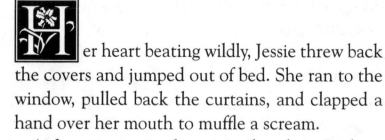er heart beating wildly, Jessie threw back the covers and jumped out of bed. She ran to the window, pulled back the curtains, and clapped a hand over her mouth to muffle a scream.

A face was pressed against the glass. Its long nose was squashed sideways. Its mouth was gaping open. Its eyes were wide with fright. There was a squeak and the face abruptly disappeared. Jessie heard a small thump.

Cautiously she opened the window and peered out. The cool night air was sweet with spring blossom. The huge trees of the Blue Moon garden whispered together beneath the starry sky. And there on the ground below the windowsill lay Giff the elf, moaning softly.

'Giff!' Jessie whispered. 'Are you all right?'

'Oh dear, oh dear!' groaned Giff, slowly sitting up and rubbing his head. 'Oh, Jessie, you gave me such a shock, looking out suddenly like that.'

'What do you expect if you go tapping on people's windows at midnight?' hissed Jessie. 'Giff, why are you here? What's wrong?'

'Everything's wrong,' Giff wailed, his pointed ears drooping so low that the tips almost touched his shoulders. 'I'm in terrible trouble, Jessie. The worst trouble *ever*. You've got to help me. You've just got to!'

'Shhh!' Jessie put her finger to her lips. 'Go back down to the secret garden, Giff. I'll meet you there. All right?'

Giff nodded miserably, and began feeling his legs and arms as if to check for bruises and broken bones.

Jessie closed the window and pulled on the clothes she'd left lying on her chair when she changed for bed. She fastened her charm bracelet around her wrist, then slipped from her room and tiptoed through the darkened house to the kitchen at the back. Granny had said she always had trouble sleeping just before Wish Night. If she *had* managed to fall asleep, Jessie didn't want to wake her.

Not unless I have to, anyway, she thought. If Giff's problem is really serious, I'll need to ask Granny's advice. But it probably isn't nearly as bad as he thinks. He's lost something or broken something, I suppose, but it can't be anything very important. No one lets Giff near anything really valuable.

She had expected the back door to be locked, as usual, but to her surprise it wasn't. Granny must have forgotten, she thought, letting herself out into the night. That's strange.

Then something else occurred to her. Granny's big ginger cat, Flynn, had surely heard her creeping through the house, but he hadn't come to investigate. Where was he?

'Hello there!' called a chirpy voice, making Jessie jump. 'What are you doing out here so late? There's nothing wrong, I hope?'

Jessie shrank back against the door. She couldn't see the owner of the voice, but she knew exactly who it was. It was Mrs Tweedie, their new next-door neighbour.

Mrs Tweedie was a small, bustling woman with

spiky grey hair, a pointed pink-tipped nose, and sharp blue eyes that darted around behind thick glasses. She reminded Jessie of a bird—a busy, curious, gossiping little bird. The Bins family, who used to live in Mrs Tweedie's house, had done their best to ignore their neighbours at Blue Moon. Mrs Tweedie did just the opposite.

She seemed to be fascinated by everything that happened next door. She was always popping in for one reason or another: to borrow something, or to ask advice, or to bring a box of cakes or biscuits, saying she'd cooked too many for herself. She spent lots of time in her garden, keeping a close eye on all the comings and goings across the fence.

Granny said Mrs Tweedie didn't have enough to do with her time. Rosemary said she was probably lonely. Jessie had started to think she was just plain nosy.

And now Mrs Tweedie had caught her sneaking out of the house at midnight! Jessie was desperately trying to think up a story to explain what she was doing when another voice floated from the garden at the front of the house.

'Oh, no, Louise. Flynn and I are just star-gazing, that's all. We enjoy it at this time of year.'

Granny! Jessie breathed a sigh of relief. So that was why the back door was unlocked. Granny was outside. Mrs Tweedie had been talking to *her*, not to Jessie at all.

'How *interesting!*' exclaimed Mrs Tweedie. 'Was your late husband, the artist, keen on—um—stargaping, too, Jessica?'

Granny laughed. 'Oh, certainly,' she said. 'Robert liked nothing better! He could gape at the stars for hours at a time.'

Jessie smothered a giggle as she crept down the back steps and onto the grass.

'I'm just back from the final Spring Fair meeting.' Mrs Tweedie was going on chattily. 'Didn't they keep us late? The Fair's on Saturday—well, you know that, of course, because it's at Jessie's school. Anyway, I heard that the organisers needed a few extra pairs of hands, so I went along to volunteer. That sort of thing's always a good way of getting to know people, isn't it?'

'Oh, yes,' said Granny. Her voice was quite friendly, but Jessie could tell that she wished Mrs Tweedie would leave her to stargaze in peace.

'Jessie's teacher, Lyn Stone, was there,' Mrs Tweedie babbled on. 'She's been organising the children's writing competition. What a *practical* young woman she is! But not what I'd call *friendly*, if you know what I mean.'

You mean she wouldn't talk to you about me, you old busybody, Jessie thought. And for once she was grateful to Ms Stone.

'That's nice,' Granny murmured vaguely. 'Well, Louise, don't let me keep you . . .'

Jessie edged quietly into the trees and ran down to the high, clipped hedge that surrounded the secret garden. She hurried through the door in the hedge, and ran straight into Giff, who was waiting just inside.

With a little squeal, Giff bounced backwards and fell flat on the grass.

'Oh, Giff, I'm so sorry!' Jessie whispered, crouching beside him and pulling him back to his feet. 'Now, quickly, tell me what happened!'

'I bumped my head,' Giff mumbled. 'You knocked me over!' He swayed. Jessie held his arm firmly.

'I don't mean what happened just now,' she whispered. 'I mean—you said you were in some sort of trouble. What trouble?'

Giff blinked in a dazed sort of way. Then he slowly raised his hand to his bulging jacket pocket and an expression of horror dawned on his face.

'Oh dear, oh dear!' he moaned. 'We have to

hurry!' And before Jessie could move or say a word, he shouted, 'Open!'

There was a sighing, whispering sound and a rush of cool wind. Jessie's skin began to tingle. Her hair flew around her head in a golden red cloud. 'N-no!' she stammered. 'No, no, Giff, I can't—'

But it was too late. Already the secret garden had disappeared and mist was swirling around Jessie's face. A moment later she felt pebbles beneath her feet and smelled warm, sweet air. She and Giff were in the Realm.

'There!' squealed a familiar voice. 'There he is, Maybelle! And Jessie's with him!'

The mist cleared from Jessie's eyes. She and Giff were on the pebbly road that ran beside the tall, dark hedge that protected the Realm. The sky above them was like black velvet sprayed with huge, twinkling diamonds.

And there, standing in front of them on the road, were Maybelle and Patrice. Maybelle was swishing her white tail crossly and pawing the ground with one hoof. Small, plump Patrice had her hands on her hips. Both of them were glaring at Giff.

'Oh, no!' wailed Giff. He clapped his hands over his eyes.

Maybelle snorted. 'Did you really think you could get away with this, you fool of an elf?' she snapped. 'The drawer's empty, and you were the only one to go to Queen Helena's room tonight, to get that box of griffin treats! Everyone else was stargazing. Come on! Where is it?'

'It's there,' Patrice sighed, pointing at Giff's bulging jacket pocket. 'Oh, Giff, how could you *do* such a thing!'

Giff whimpered.

'Patrice—Maybelle—what's happening?' Jessie burst out in confusion. 'What's Giff done?'

'*Done?*' fumed Maybelle. 'Oh, nothing much. He's only stuffed the most precious thing in the Realm into his grubby pocket and run away. He's only made off with Queen Helena's Star Cloak, the night before Wish Night, that's all!'

'I didn't make off with the Star Cloak!' Giff wailed, taking his hands away from his eyes. 'I just—borrowed it. I was going to bring it back when . . . when . . .'

'I knew it!' exclaimed Patrice. 'I just *knew* you'd taken it to show Jessie. When we discovered it was missing, Maybelle and I rushed straight here. Oh!' She fanned her hot face with her hand. 'I'm so relieved we found you! You're just very lucky

that no one knows about this but us. All right—
give it to me.'

She held out her small, brown hand. But Giff
clutched at his pocket, shrank back against Jessie,
and shook his head.

'Giff!' thundered Maybelle. 'Give—the Star
Cloak—to—Patrice!'

Giff just kept shaking his head. Jessie could
feel him trembling. She put her arm around his
quivering shoulders and frowned. Something was
very wrong here, and she had a horrible feeling
that she knew what it was.

CHAPTER THREE

The Cloak

ou didn't really take the Star Cloak just to show me, did you, Giff?' Jessie asked gently.

'No,' Giff moaned. 'I wanted . . . I wanted you to come with me, Jessie. I was too scared to go on my own.'

'What are you babbling about?' demanded Maybelle. 'Too scared to go *where* on your own?'

Patrice wasn't listening. Her small black eyes were fixed on Giff's hands, which were still clutched protectively over his pocket. Patrice suspects what I suspect, Jessie thought, and her heart sank.

'Why won't you give me the Star Cloak, Giff?'

Patrice asked in a level voice.

Giff's eyes widened in terror.

'Something awful's happened,' Patrice went on. 'I feel it in my bones. Come on, Giff, you might as well tell us. The Cloak's been damaged, hasn't it?'

'What?' roared Maybelle. '*Damaged!*'

Giff suddenly went limp. His hands dropped to his sides. His ears drooped miserably. 'It wasn't my fault,' he whispered. 'I found the griffin treats in a drawer, and as I was getting them out, I pulled another drawer open by mistake. The Star Cloak was there, in its bag. And I—I just thought I'd have a peep at it. Just a tiny peep, Patrice. But the Cloak was rolled up so tightly that I couldn't really see it. So . . . so . . .'

'So you took it out of the bag,' Patrice said grimly. 'You unrolled it. And then—'

Giff burst into tears. 'I didn't mean it to happen!' He sobbed. 'I was just looking. It was so beautiful! It swirled around me like tingly spiderwebs. I don't know how my foot got caught in it. But somehow it did, and I got all tangled up, and I fell over, and there was this awful, tearing sound and—'

'Don't say any more,' said Maybelle, closing her eyes. She tossed her head at Patrice. 'Get it,' she ordered. 'We may as well know the worst.'

Patrice pulled a small black velvet bag from Giff's jacket pocket. Giff sobbed even harder, but made no move to stop her.

Jessie watched, fascinated, as Patrice untied the bag's silver drawstrings, pulled the bag open, and slowly drew out a little roll of shimmering, pale blue cloth.

But that can't be the Cloak, Jessie thought. It's much too small. Then she gasped as Patrice held the roll high and shook it out.

The Star Cloak billowed free, floating in the sweet night air. It sparkled like blue and silver starlight, delicate as a fairy's wing, light as spun gossamer, glimmering with magic.

But right in the centre of the back, running almost to the hem, was an ugly, gaping tear. Even as the friends watched, a few sparkling threads drifted away from the tear and floated towards the ground.

Patrice drew a sharp breath. Maybelle drew her lips back from her teeth. Giff buried his face in his hands. 'I put the Cloak on and wished the tear would go away,' he wailed. 'But it didn't work. The tear just got bigger!'

'I can't believe this has happened,' Patrice murmured at last. 'This Cloak was new last year.

It's not due to be replaced till the next blue moon—and that's—that's forty-nine years from now!' She was very pale. Her plump hands trembled as she gently rolled up the Cloak again. 'Oh, how can Queen Helena wear the Cloak like this?'

'She can't!' Maybelle said shortly. 'The threads won't stay in place now that they're torn, you know that, Patrice. If Queen Helena wears the Cloak tomorrow night, there'll be nothing left of it by dawn. No, there's nothing to be done. Wish Night will have to be cancelled.'

'But crowds from the farthest parts of the Realm are already on their way!' cried Patrice. 'By the time we can spread the word, most of them will have arrived at the palace. And all so excited, in their best clothes, with their wishes ready—'

Giff gave an agonised, muffled groan.

'But surely the whole of Wish Night doesn't have to be cancelled just because the Star Cloak is torn!' Jessie exclaimed. 'Surely Queen Helena has other beautiful clothes she could wear.'

As soon as the words left her mouth she realised she'd said something stupid. Patrice, Maybelle and even Giff were staring at her in astonishment.

'The Star Cloak *is* Wish Night, dearie,' Patrice said gently after a moment. 'Didn't you know? It's the Star Cloak's magic that makes the stars fall. If Queen Helena doesn't wear it . . . well, nothing will happen at all.'

'Oh,' said Jessie weakly. 'I didn't realise.' For the first time, she understood that Giff had been speaking the truth when he'd said he was in the worst trouble ever.

'No point in standing here talking,' Maybelle muttered. 'We'd better go and tell Queen Helena.'

'No!' wailed Giff, throwing himself on the ground. 'No, no, no, no, no! You can't tell *anyone*! And Wish Night *can't* be cancelled. Everyone will blame me! Everyone will hate me! No one will ever speak to me again!'

'Oh, I daresay they'll forgive you eventually,' Maybelle said curtly. 'In a hundred years or so.' She tossed her mane. 'If you live that long,' she added. 'Which I doubt, if the griffins get to hear of this.'

Giff burst into tears again.

Jessie felt so sorry for him. It had been very wrong of him to touch the Star Cloak. But the results had been so terrible that surely he'd been punished enough. He'd run to her for help—but so far she'd done nothing for him at all.

Then she remembered something he'd said. 'Giff,' she murmured. 'You said you wanted me to go somewhere with you—somewhere you were afraid to go alone. Where was that?'

'S-Stardust Mountain.' Giff sobbed. 'That's w-where the Star Cloak was made. The star fairies there could mend it; I know they could. I thought—I thought if we could get there and back by tomorrow morning, no one would ever have to know. But now—'

'Stardust Mountain indeed!' snorted Maybelle. 'Are you out of your mind? Even if the star fairies didn't sting you to death when they saw what you'd done to a Star Cloak that took them *fifty years* to make, how did you think you and Jessie could get to the Mountain and back in a single night?'

Giff took a shuddering breath. 'I thought we could use the Cloak,' he said. 'I thought we could put it around us, very carefully, and wish. Queen Helena told me that whoever wears the Cloak can make wishes anytime, not just on Wish Night. All you have to do is wish for the thing you want most in the world. The wish has to be possible, and there have to be stars in the sky. Going to Star Mountain *is* possible, and there are lots of stars tonight.'

There was a short silence. Then Patrice and Maybelle glanced at each other.

'It could work, you know,' Patrice said slowly. 'And it would solve everything.'

'Have you ever seen a star fairy in a temper, Patrice?' Maybelle retorted.

Patrice frowned. 'Very nasty,' she agreed. 'But maybe . . .'

She turned to Jessie, who was staring at them, wide-eyed. 'It's like this, dearie,' she said carefully. 'The fairies on Stardust Mountain are a bit touchy, if you know what I mean.'

'A *bit* touchy?' snorted Maybelle.

'They have to be approached in just the right way or there's trouble,' Patrice went on, flapping a hand at Maybelle to quiet her. 'Not that they're *bad*, you understand. But they're very secretive, and they don't like strangers coming to the Mountain. I was thinking that if *you* were with us, Jessie, they might be so interested to meet you that they'd keep their tempers and fix the Cloak for us, too.'

'That's what I thought!' Giff snuffled, wiping his eyes and climbing to his feet. 'That's why I wanted Jessie to come with me.'

Patrice frowned at him. 'How you could even

think of taking Jessie to Stardust Mountain with only you to look after her, I do not know!' she snapped. 'It's very lucky we caught you in time. If we go, we'll all go together.'

'And it had better be soon,' muttered Maybelle, glancing at the sky. 'The night's not getting any younger. What do you say, Jessie? Will you come with us?'

Jessie hesitated. If she agreed to go to Stardust Mountain, she'd be away from home all night. She wouldn't get any sleep at all!

She thought of school tomorrow, and Ms Stone. Then she looked at Giff's tear-stained face and pleading eyes and knew that there was only one choice she could make. 'Of course I'll go with you,' she said warmly. 'As long as I can be back by the time Mum gets home from work in the morning, I'd be happy to help.'

CHAPTER FOUR

Stardust Mountain

'We'll be back from Stardust Mountain long before your mother gets home, Jessie,' said Patrice, patting Jessie's arm. 'We'll have to be, whatever happens. It would be terribly dangerous to have a Star Cloak outdoors after dawn.'

'One ray of sunlight will destroy it,' Maybelle explained, seeing Jessie's confused expression. 'Well, what would you expect? It *is* made of woven stardust and moonbeams.'

Jessie's jaw dropped.

'I thought you knew, dearie!' exclaimed Patrice. 'The star fairy workers spin dust from falling stars with beams from the blue moon to make the threads. Then they weave the threads together to make the cloth. That's why the Cloak's so magic, and so precious. The black velvet bag gives it some protection, of course, but we wouldn't want to take any risks.'

'We'd better get moving, then, hadn't we?' said Maybelle bossily. 'Now, Jessie, you'll wear the Cloak, because you're the tallest—'

'And, besides, it's only right!' Patrice put in. 'Jessie *is* Queen Jessica's granddaughter.'

Maybelle rolled her eyes. 'That, too,' she said. 'Giff, you stand beside Jessie. When the Cloak's in place, Patrice can get on the other side, and I'll stand in front. We all have to be covered completely before we wish, and while we're travelling. When I give the signal, we all think, "I wish I were with the fairies on Stardust Mountain", and really mean it. Is that understood?'

'Of course it's understood, Maybelle!' snapped Patrice as she handed the black velvet bag to Jessie and began unrolling the Star Cloak once more. 'We're not silly.'

'Some of us are,' said Maybelle darkly, shooting a glance at Giff.

Jessie tucked the bag into her pocket and held out her arm. Giff shot to her side and snuggled against her. Patrice draped the floating blue folds of the Cloak around both of them.

Jessie shivered. The Cloak was as light as air, but she could feel a cool tingling all over her body, right through her clothes. She could hear Giff's teeth chattering.

'It's cold!' Giff whimpered.

'Yes, Queen Helena always says that,' said Patrice as she stood on her toes and started tying the Cloak's silver strings at Jessie's neck. 'And I remember her dear mother saying it before her. Ah, well. Magic isn't always comfortable.'

'I can hear something!' Maybelle said sharply.

Patrice stiffened, listening intently. 'Someone's coming along the road!' she whispered. 'From the direction of the palace, too. It sounds like . . . Oh, Maybelle, it sounds like—'

'What?' cried Giff in panic from beneath the Cloak.

'It sounds like a troop of guards,' Maybelle hissed. 'Get those strings tied, Patrice!'

'I'm trying!' panted Patrice, fumbling with the silver strings. 'You know how slippery they are. And if they aren't tied properly we'll lose the Cloak on the way. Oh, paddywinks and sosslebones! I keep losing my grip.'

'This is a disaster!' Maybelle growled.

Now Jessie, too, could hear the marching feet coming towards them. She couldn't see anything, because of a bend in the road, but the sounds were becoming louder and louder. At any moment the troop would round the bend and see them.

'Hurry, Patrice!' she whispered.

'Troop—halt!' a guard yelled, and the marching feet stopped.

'That's Loris's voice,' Maybelle muttered. 'It must be something important for *his* troop to be sent out. They weren't on duty tonight. The last I saw of them they were stargazing with everyone else.'

'You there!' they heard Loris roar. 'You rabbits under that tree—yes, you, with the daisies behind your ears! Have you seen an elf come by here?'

Jessie's stomach turned over. She heard Giff whimper beneath the Cloak and pressed his hand comfortingly. Patrice grunted with effort as she wrestled with the silver strings.

'Well?' called Loris, more loudly.

'We 'aven't done nuffin',' a snuffly voice called back. 'We 'aven't done nuffin', an' we don't know about nuffin'. 'Cept grass.'

'An' daisies,' a squeakier voice put in.

'An' daisies,' the snuffly voice repeated loudly. 'We don't know about nuffin' but grass and daisies.'

'An' carrots,' said the squeaky voice. 'An' lettuce. An'—'

There was a loud chorus of snuffly, shushing sounds.

'It's no good asking them anything, Loris,' snapped a guard's voice. 'They've got nothing but fluff between the ears.'

'That's rude, that is!' retorted the first rabbit. 'We could report you for that!'

'We could report *you* for being deliberately unhelpful!' snapped Loris. 'Have you seen an elf, or not?'

'Maybe we 'ave, and maybe we 'aven't,' said the first rabbit, with a sniff. 'Maybe 'e came runnin' down the road here, red in the face and puffin' like a walrus, with somefin' big stuffed in 'is pocket, and maybe 'e didn't. We'll never tell you lot, any'ow!'

'The silly thing has told them already!' hissed Patrice.

'Troop!' roared Loris at the same moment. 'Quick march!'

'Oh, no!' squeaked Giff. 'They're coming!

They'll catch me! Oh! Oh! I wish we were in Stardust Mountain with the star fairies!'

Instantly Jessie's skin felt cold as ice. A blue light flamed before her eyes. She heard Patrice scream. Then everything went dark.

When she woke, she was shivering. She had no idea how much time had passed. She opened her eyes and saw tiny flashing lights swirling around her. An angry humming filled her ears. Quickly she shut her eyes again.

Slowly her mind began working. She felt the cool, tingling folds of the Star Cloak wrapped around her. She remembered that Giff had panicked and wished them to Stardust Mountain, leaving Patrice and Maybelle behind. But where was Giff now? She couldn't feel him, or hear him. All she could hear was that strange buzzing sound . . .

She forced her eyes open again. She was lying on her back. Tiny lights were still whirling above her. Beyond them were other lights—thousands of stars twinkling in the night sky. They looked so close that Jessie felt she could touch them if she stretched out her hand.

But the whirling lights were even closer. They were swooping low over her upturned face, buzzing like a swarm of bees. And then Jessie saw that they weren't lights, but tiny fairies whose pale skin glowed and sparkled.

There were hundreds of them. They had long, silky, pale blue hair, and their robes were silver, blue and mauve. Their wings were whirring so fast that they made a humming sound. Their pointed faces did not look friendly.

The star fairies, Jessie thought fearfully.

The fairies at the front of the swarm were larger than the rest. They were scowling. Their long, white fingers, tipped with nails as sharp as needles, were jabbing the air. 'Who are you, human girl?' they were crying in tiny, buzzing voices. 'Why have you come to our Mountain? How did you dare to use the Star Cloak? Explain! Explain! Explain!'

Jessie cleared her throat. 'I am Jessie, granddaughter of Jessica, the Realm's true queen,' she managed to say. 'I have come to ask you—'

'Jessie!' some of the smaller fairies cried excitedly. 'Queen Helena told us of Jessie! Jessie saved the Realm last year, at the time of the blue moon!'

Chattering, they tried to press forward, but the larger fairies at the front held them back. Jessie decided that the larger fairies must be the swarm's soldiers. Their fierce expressions had not changed, and they still held their thornlike nails at the ready.

'She *says* she is Jessie, but she offers us no proof,' one of them droned. 'I think she lies! Why would the granddaughter of Queen Jessica come here without warning, and with no royal guards to protect her? And why would Queen Helena let the Star Cloak out of her sight, the night before Wish Night?'

'Warrior Flash is right,' another said. 'We must think of this further.'

'We do not need to think further!' buzzed the fierce fairy called Flash, jabbing at Jessie with her pointed nails. 'We should sting her, sting her until she tells the truth!'

'No!' Jessie cried desperately. 'I really *am* Jessie, I am! Ask Giff—the elf who came with me. He'll tell you I'm not lying!'

'No one came with you,' snapped Flash, her frown deepening. 'What trick are you playing?'

Jessie felt a stab of fear. Giff must have fallen from under the Star Cloak as they reached Stardust Mountain. He was lost somewhere on the Mountain, and she was here alone.

'She is an invader!' cried Flash. 'Warriors, attack!'

And instantly all the soldier fairies dived straight at Jessie, their needle-sharp nails glinting in the light.

CHAPTER FIVE

Flash and Gleam

essie screamed and flung her arms over her face. Dimly she heard her charm bracelet jingling on her wrist. She thought of her mother, of Granny, of Giff, Patrice, Maybelle, Queen Helena. They can't help me, she thought in terror. No one can help me. . . .

Then she realised that the angry buzzing had stopped. It had changed to a low humming. And the star fairies had not touched her.

Cautiously she moved her arms a little, and opened her eyes. She saw that the swarm was circling over her charm bracelet.

'You see!' one of the smaller fairies cried. 'She *is*

Jessie! She wears the golden bracelet, hung with Realm gifts, just as Queen Helena told us. It is the proof! The proof!'

The humming swarm drew back until it was hovering at a respectful distance. The warriors put their hands behind their backs, as if to show they were no longer a threat.

Weak with relief, Jessie sat up. She saw that she was on a high mountaintop, surrounded by big rocks and clusters of sweet-smelling plants. Huge stars blazed above her, and everything was bathed in a strange, magical light. Wondering where the light was coming from, Jessie glanced behind her. There, not far above where she was sitting, was the very tip of the Mountain. Cool, white light was streaming from it, flooding the rocks below.

Jessie shivered and huddled further into the folds of the Star Cloak. But the slippery, magic cloth did not warm her any more than the light did.

The star fairies had been talking seriously to one another. Now they fell silent, and one lonely figure flew forward. As it came closer, Jessie saw that it was the soldier fairy, Warrior Flash.

'We beg your pardon, Jessie,' said Flash stiffly. 'The fault was mine, for I ordered the attack. I await my punishment. My life is yours to take.'

'Oh . . . no!' Jessie exclaimed. 'I don't want to hurt you.'

A great buzzing rose from the listening swarm. There was a whirr of wings, and the next moment, the smaller fairies were dancing in the air in front of Jessie, their faces bright with relief. She held out her hands to them and dozens of them landed on her fingers, chattering and laughing. But the soldiers kept their distance, looking wary and puzzled.

'I thank you for sparing me,' Flash said slowly. 'I do not understand your reasons, however. You do not seem to be a weakling.'

'Clearly Jessie is no weakling,' one of the other soldier fairies agreed. 'She showed courage when we attacked. She could have used the Star Cloak to escape us, but she did not. Her mission here must be of great importance.'

Jessie looked up quickly. Of course! she thought. I'm wearing the Star Cloak, so I could have just wished myself away from here. I was just so confused and frightened that I completely forgot!

She opened her mouth to say this, then changed her mind. The star fairy warriors seemed to value strength and courage above everything else. It would be best not to admit to any weakness.

She crawled to her feet. The little fairies in her hands flew upwards in a shining cloud. She felt the cool folds of the Star Cloak float around her and took a deep breath. 'My mission *is* important,' she said, keeping her voice as calm and level as she could. 'I'm afraid the Cloak is damaged.' She turned around so that the fairies could see the ragged tear.

A loud, horrified buzzing rose from the swarm. Then Jessie felt the breeze of whirring wings, and her spine tingled as hundreds of tiny hands touched the damaged Cloak.

'Take it off! Take it off!' the fairies cried frantically. 'Every moment more threads drift free, and the damage grows worse!'

Jessie felt for the silver strings and untied them. The Cloak slipped from her shoulders. She turned and saw it being swept away through the air, completely covered by the smaller fairies and surrounded by the warriors. Only Flash remained, hovering before her.

'Where are they taking it?' Jessie asked anxiously.

'To the Cavern,' said Flash sternly, pointing over

Jessie's head to the glowing tip of the Mountain. 'There the Oldest One will decide if mending is possible. Did *you* damage the Star Cloak?'

'No,' Jessie said, very glad that it was the truth.

'Then name the culprit!' Flash buzzed. 'The enemy who tore the Cloak must be found and punished.'

'There is no enemy,' exclaimed Jessie. 'It was an accident.'

Flash's sharp eyes narrowed. 'When you arrived, you said that an elf called Giff was with you,' she said coldly. 'But you were alone. I think this Giff damaged the Cloak, then was too afraid to show his face here, because he knew what we would do. No doubt he is hiding somewhere on the Mountain. When the other warriors return, we will begin the hunt for him.'

Filled with dismay, Jessie turned away so Flash couldn't see her face. But she knew it was too late. The fairy had already guessed part of the truth, and now Giff was in terrible danger.

I have to stop them from going after him, Jessie thought. I have to give him time to get away from the Mountain. Even if he's captured by the palace guards, that would be much better than being caught by the star fairies.

'I don't think you should go hunting anyone, Flash,' she said aloud. 'You and the others should stay here to protect the Cloak.'

There was silence for a moment. Jessie didn't turn around. Again she looked up at the tip of the Mountain. Now she could see that the light she had noticed before was streaming from the mouth of a huge cave. The light flowed over her, beautiful but cold, and suddenly she longed for the sun.

At last Flash spoke again. 'I know that for some reason you want to save this elf from the punishment he deserves,' she said. 'But still, what you say is true. The Cloak must be guarded, so the search must wait. There is no great hurry, anyway. Strangers lost on the Mountain never escape it without help. There are too many cliffs and holes for that.'

Jessie thought of poor Giff, lost and alone. He was never very brave at any time. What must he be feeling now? Don't panic, Giff, she told him in her mind. Don't do anything silly or dangerous. The moment I get the Star Cloak back, I'll wish I was with you. Then I'll wish us both back to the palace.

Her heart thudded as she saw three glowing specks shoot from the cavern's mouth and hurtle down towards them. Three of the soldier fairies were returning. What news would they bring? What if they said the Star Cloak was beyond repair? What if they said it would take days, or even weeks, to mend?

The three newcomers stopped directly in front of her. 'The news is good,' said the largest of the three. 'The Cloak can be mended. The work has already begun. It will take many hours, but will be finished before the last star has faded from the sky.'

A wave of relief flowed over Jessie. 'Oh, I'm so glad!' she cried. 'So *glad!*'

The soldier fairy nodded. 'We, too, are glad,' he said gravely. 'The Oldest One has invited you to wait in the Cavern while—'

'None but the star fairies may enter the Cavern, Warrior Gleam,' Flash snapped. 'Even Queen Helena and Princess Christie remained outside when they came a year ago to accept the new Cloak. You must be mistaken.'

Gleam calmly shook his head. 'I am not mistaken,' he said. 'The Oldest One reminds us that our mountaintop is too cold for Folk to remain on for long without harm. The same is true of humans. The Oldest One does not want

Jessie to become ill, for who then would return the Cloak to the Queen?'

Flash thought for a moment, then nodded. 'Follow!' she ordered Jessie. Then she began to fly upwards, a floating glimmer of light. Gleam and the other fairies went with her, their long, fine hair drifting around their heads in pale blue clouds. They looked so beautiful, and so delicate, it was hard to believe that they could harm anyone—or want to.

It just goes to show that you can't judge people by what they look like, Jessie thought, climbing after her guides. If it hadn't been for the charm bracelet, they would have stung me to death without a shred of pity.

As they drew closer to the tip of the Mountain, the humming sound grew louder, the light grew brighter, and the magic in the air became so strong that Jessie's skin was prickling with it. She began to climb faster.

Flash, Gleam and their companions reached the cave and hovered at the entrance, almost invisible in the radiant glow. Jessie arrived at their side, panting, and only then realised that all the other star fairy warriors were at the Cavern's mouth, too. The light was filled with hundreds of small, flying figures with fierce faces and needle-sharp nails.

'We will enter,' Flash said loudly. 'It is the will of the Oldest One.'

The warrior fairies moved aside, putting their hands behind their backs to show that they would not strike.

Her heart pounding, her eyes watering in the light, Jessie moved through the entrance, and into the Cavern.

CHAPTER SIX

The Cavern

he Cavern was huge and echoing. Its corners were dim, but its centre was glowing with light. Hundreds of star fairies were gathered there, working on the damaged Star Cloak, which floated, glittering, a little way off the floor.

Fairies were clustered thickly along both sides of the long, ragged tear, their wings humming, their fingers flying as they wove loose threads together. Other fairies, their hands filled with shining blue and silver, were flying up and down along the centre of the tear, dropping new threads to workers who needed them.

'Are those threads really made of stardust and

moonbeams?' Jessie whispered.

'Of course,' said Gleam, who was flying just in front of her. 'They have been spun for the next Star Cloak, but the Oldest One has ordered that as many as are needed can be used for the mending.'

'You should not speak,' muttered Flash, from Jessie's other side. 'The workers must not be disturbed. We will take Jessie to the rest chamber, Warrior Gleam. She will sleep there, and cause no trouble.'

'The Oldest One has asked to see her, Warrior Flash,' said Gleam. 'The Oldest One is curious to see the granddaughter of Queen Jessica.'

Flash buzzed sullenly, but did not argue. This fairy they call the Oldest One must be their leader, Jessie thought. She felt nervous as she followed the two soldier fairies around the mass of working fairies and into the most brilliant part of the light.

There, a chair of woven grass hung high above the ground, suspended by sparkling threads. In the chair, watching the work being done below, sat the most ancient fairy Jessie had ever seen. Her flowing hair was silver-white. Her tiny face and hands looked almost transparent, as if they were made of pure light. But her robes were a deep, rich blue, and her grey eyes were filled with interest as she looked up and caught sight of Jessie.

Jessie bowed awkwardly, too nervous to speak.

'You look very like your grandmother,' the old fairy said in a harsh, cracked voice. 'It is good to see you here, though what you brought with you gave us pain.'

Her eyes moved from Jessie's face down to the damaged Star Cloak. Suddenly she frowned. 'Worker Glitter!' she called sharply. 'You have missed a thread! Undo your work and begin again!'

A small fairy in blue jumped, ducked her head, and began plucking nervously at a group of threads so tiny that Jessie couldn't even see them.

The Oldest One sighed. 'The young workers need watching every moment,' she said. 'The mending must be done speedily, that is true, but still it must be done well. This Star Cloak must last through the coming Wish Night, and forty-eight other Wish Nights, too, before a new Cloak can be ready to replace it.'

'So—so Star Cloaks really *do* take fifty whole years to make?' stammered Jessie, finding her voice at last. 'Is that because there's only a blue moon once every fifty years?'

'No,' said the Oldest One, without taking her eyes off the workers. 'We can always gather more than enough blue moonbeams to store for our purposes. Stardust is another matter.' She moved restlessly in her chair. 'It takes a great deal of stardust to make a Star Cloak. It is hard to gather as much as we need, even in fifty years.'

'How do you gather it?' Jessie asked, fascinated. Flash buzzed angrily in her ear, and even Gleam made an uncomfortable sound, but the Oldest One only smiled.

'You are as full of questions as your grandmother was when she visited us,' she said. 'And I will answer you, just as I answered her, long ago.'

She pointed upwards. Jessie looked up and was startled to see, high above her, a vast gap in the Cavern roof. Beyond the gap was the brilliance of the night sky.

'During the day, when we sleep, the sky window is covered, to protect our work,' the old fairy explained. 'But at night it is always open, to catch the dust of any star that falls above our Mountain. The dust sweeps in like shining snow, attracted by the stardust we already have. And we gather it, gather it as fast as we can, in silken bags, and add it to our store.'

Jessie thought for a moment. 'Stars don't fall very often, except on Wish Night,' she said slowly. 'So Wish Night must be a very important night for you, every year.'

'*Important?*' The Oldest One gave a harsh, buzzing laugh that had little humour in it. 'You could say that! Why do you think we agreed to put aside our work to mend the damaged Cloak so quickly?'

She frowned, tapping her tiny fingers, waiting for an answer.

'So . . . so that Wish Night won't have to be cancelled,' said Jessie uncertainly. 'So that the stars will still fall. And so you—'

'So we will survive!' snapped the Oldest One. 'If we miss even one Wish Night, we will not have enough stardust to finish the new Star Cloak by the time the old Cloak fades at the next blue moon. The magic line will be broken. There will be no new Star Cloak. There will be no more Wish Nights.'

Her eyes darkened. Her hands clenched into fists. 'And if the Star Cloaks end, so does the star fairies' purpose,' she said. 'Our work is our life. If the Star Cloaks end, we, too, will fade away.'

Jessie gasped in horror.

'Leave me now,' the Oldest One said abruptly. 'Your likeness to your grandmother made me show weakness. I have told you too many of our secrets already. Keep them to yourself, if you value our friendship.'

Flash and Gleam tweaked Jessie's hair, urging her away. Jessie stumbled back, bowed again to the Oldest One, then followed the two fairies as they led her to a shadowy corner of the Cavern.

She was horrified by what she had heard. Patrice, Maybelle and Giff don't know about this, she thought. They were only worried about the Realm people being disappointed if Wish Night was cancelled. They don't realise that missing one Wish Night would mean the end of the Star Cloaks, and the star fairies, too.

She remembered the Oldest One's last, mumbled words. *I have told you too many of our secrets already . . .*

The star fairies hate to admit to any weakness, Jessie thought. They don't trust anyone to understand them, so they've always kept their troubles secret. I might be the only person in the Realm—except maybe Queen Helena—to know how important every Wish Night is to them.

'You can wait in here.' Flash's sharp voice cut

through Jessie's thoughts. She looked up and saw that her guides were hovering in front of an archway that led into another, smaller cave.

'I am not sure that the workers' rest chamber is the best place for Jessie to wait, Warrior Flash,' Gleam said quietly. 'Jessie is not even of the Folk. She is human.'

'No lasting harm will come to her, Warrior Gleam!' Flash snapped. 'And I must be certain that she will not find a way to creep out of the Cavern to find Giff the elf and help him to escape. Leave us now. You are needed at the entrance.'

Gleam hesitated, his face creased in concern. Then he bowed his head and flew quickly away.

Jessie looked anxiously into the dimness beyond the archway. She couldn't see anything. 'Couldn't I just wait here, at the side of the Cavern?' she asked in a low voice. 'I wouldn't try to creep out, I promise. I've got no idea where Giff is. I couldn't find him, even if I tried!'

'You must wait in the rest chamber,' Flash said harshly. 'We will call you when the Cloak is ready.'

Jessie knew it would be useless to argue any more. Nervously, wishing she knew why Gleam had been so worried, she moved into the cave.

It was warmer than the great Cavern had been, and the air was heavy with a tangy scent that reminded Jessie of the rosemary bushes in the secret garden.

Gradually her eyes grew used to the dimness and she saw that thick couches of dried leaves lined the cave walls. That's where the perfume's coming from, she thought. The couches. The leaves . . .

She hadn't felt sleepy before, but suddenly her eyelids felt very heavy—so heavy that she could hardly keep them open. Almost without noticing what she was doing, she moved to the nearest couch and lay down. The leaves cushioned her in rustling, fragrant softness.

Something in this cave makes you sleep, she realised hazily. The scent of the leaves, maybe. Or just magic. That's why Flash wanted me here. And that's why Gleam was worried. This place is meant for star fairies, not for Folk, or humans. That's why . . .

But she never finished the thought. Her eyes closed, and in seconds she was fast asleep.

CHAPTER SEVEN

Dreams

essie was dreaming of the secret garden. The rosemary bushes were humming with bees. The tall, green hedge seemed to keep the whole world out. She felt wonderfully happy and peaceful.

The humming of the bees grew louder, and suddenly there was a sharp buzz right beside her ear. One of the bees had come too close. She tried to brush it away. The buzzing didn't stop. And now it was starting to sound like a voice—a tiny voice, calling her anxiously.

Jessie frowned. She didn't want to listen to the voice. She didn't want to leave the secret garden where she felt so happy and safe.

'I *told* you it was dangerous to leave her here, Warrior Flash!' the little voice said. 'The resting magic is too strong for humans.'

'Jessie, *get up!*' raged another voice, and Jessie felt her hair being pulled painfully. She forced her eyes open. Through a sleepy haze she saw two small, shining figures hovering in front of her. She crawled to her feet and stood swaying and blinking in confusion.

'Jessie, the Cloak is ready, but the stars are fading,' buzzed the second voice. 'Come quickly!'

Star fairies, Jessie thought dreamily. They want me to go with them. But I don't want to. I want to go back to the secret garden.

Tiny hands tugged at her hair again. Slowly it came to Jessie that the little creatures wouldn't leave her alone until she'd done what they wanted her to do. She followed them out of the dimness and into a huge cavern that glowed with light and echoed with a humming sound.

I've been here before, Jessie thought, but she couldn't remember when or why. She stumbled after her guides till she stood below a great gap in the cavern roof. Through the gap she could see a single star glimmering faintly in a pale gray sky. It looked very far away—far away, and cold. She remembered the light and warmth of the secret garden. That was better, she thought. Much better . . .

'Put on the Cloak, Jessie!' an old, cracked voice ordered. 'Make haste! Only one star remains. When it fades, it will be too late to wish, and the Cloak will not be returned in time. Workers, help her!'

Jessie felt something cool and tingling float onto her shoulders. She heard the whirring of wings, and felt tiny, clever fingers fastening strings at her neck. Soon, she thought, her eyelids drooping. Soon . . .

'Beware, Oldest One!' a voice called urgently. 'The girl is still half asleep. She—'

'Be silent, Warrior Gleam!' snapped the old voice. 'There is no time! The Cloak is tied, Jessie. Make your wish and go!'

At last, Jessie thought drowsily. She let her eyes close, and wished with all her heart that she was back in the secret garden.

Jessie woke to the sound of birds calling. She lay still

for a moment, eyes closed, enjoying the memory of the lovely dream she'd just had. She'd been in the secret garden, perfectly happy. Someone had made her leave it, but then she'd been able to return. It had been wonderful.

She shivered, and slowly realised that she was cold, and that the softness beneath her cheek was damp. She opened her eyes and stared around her in confusion. She really *was* in the secret garden, lying on the grass in the shadow of the tall hedge. How had this happened?

And suddenly memory flooded back. The Star Cloak! She'd taken the Star Cloak to be mended, but . . . Panic-stricken, she touched the cool folds of the Star Cloak, still wrapped around her. She sat bolt upright and looked wildly up at the sky. It arched over her, blue with just a trace of white cloud. And the sun . . . the sun!

A golden pool of sunlight was lying in the entrance to the secret garden. The pool was growing by the moment, moving towards her as the sun climbed higher in the sky. It had nearly reached her—nearly reached the Star Cloak.

Maybelle's voice echoed in her mind. *One ray of sunlight will destroy it. One ray of sunlight will . . .*

Frantically Jessie tore at the silver strings that

tied the Cloak. They slipped beneath her fingers. The sunlight was stealing closer. She gathered the Cloak around her and scrambled back. Forcing herself to be calm, she pulled at the strings again, and this time managed to untie them.

She stood up and pulled the Cloak from her shoulders. It floated in her hands, drifting in the air like spiderweb. The sunlight had almost reached her feet. She backed away from it, frantically rolling the folds of the Cloak into a tight package. Turning her back to the sunlight, she felt in her pocket for the black velvet bag, hoping desperately that she had not lost it.

The bag was there. Jessie pulled it out and stuffed the Star Cloak inside. She forced the bag deep into her pocket again, and breathed a sigh of relief. The Cloak was safe. Now all she had to do was go through the Door to the Realm and return it to the palace.

'Jessie! What on earth are you doing out here so early?'

Jessie jumped violently and spun around, covering her bulging pocket with her hands. Her mother was standing at the entrance to the secret garden. She was wearing an overcoat over her nurse's uniform and looked very tired.

'Oh—hi, Mum,' Jessie said weakly. 'You're home!'

'And what a welcome I got!' Rosemary said, shaking her head and smiling. 'No tea in the pot, Granny fast asleep, and you gone.' She beckoned. 'Don't just stand there, Jessie! You should be getting ready for school.'

Jessie found her voice at last. 'I—I'll come in a minute, Mum,' she said.

'Oh no,' said Rosemary firmly. 'If I leave you, you'll start daydreaming again.'

'Mum, just a few more minutes,' Jessie pleaded. 'I promise I'll—'

'Jessie, it's been a long night,' her mother said, sighing. 'Just come, will you?'

Jessie knew there was no point in arguing. What am I going to do? she thought desperately as she followed her mother out of the secret garden and up to the house. I've got to tell someone about poor Giff. And I've got to get the Cloak back to Queen Helena! Oh, why did I wish myself back here, instead of to the palace? How could I have been so stupid?

She clenched her fists, and forced herself to be calm. She knew that panic wouldn't help. If I get changed and have breakfast really quickly, maybe Mum will stop worrying about me and I'll be able to slip down to the secret garden again, she thought. If that doesn't work, I'll hide the Star Cloak somewhere and tell Granny about it. She doesn't go to the Realm very often, but she'd do it for an emergency like this.

She realised that she'd reached the back steps, and that Rosemary was opening the door and going into the kitchen. Jessie was suddenly very aware of the big bulge the Star Cloak made in her pocket. So far her mother hadn't noticed it, but as soon as they were inside she'd see it and ask about it for sure.

Panic started to rise in Jessie all over again. Then she saw a basket of clothes just inside the back door. Rosemary had her back turned, and was pulling off her coat. Quickly Jessie dragged the Star Cloak bag out of her pocket and stuffed it deep into the basket.

Just in time. Rosemary turned around. 'You need a haircut, Jessie,' she murmured, brushing the hair out of Jessie's eyes. Her hand dropped to Jessie's shoulder and she drew back, frowning in concern. 'You're all damp!' she exclaimed, patting Jessie's clothes. 'Don't tell me you've been lying on the wet grass? Oh, Jessie, what am I going to do with

66

you? Go and get out of those things straightaway. And you'd better have a quick shower to warm yourself up. You're freezing!'

Jessie scuttled off to her room and grabbed her school clothes. As she hurried to the bathroom, she heard her mother talking to someone. Who could be visiting this early? She listened curiously, then recognised the second voice. It was Mrs Tweedie from next door.

She's made some excuse to come in, Jessie thought crossly, moving quickly on to the bathroom. I'll bet she's dying to ask Mum about Granny watching the stars in the middle of the night.

She showered and changed in record time, and in ten minutes she was back in the kitchen. Her mother, who was sitting at the table, drinking tea, raised her eyebrows in surprise. 'That was quick,' she said.

Jessie forced a smile and nodded. She put some cereal into a bowl and grabbed a spoon. Then she sat down at the table with her mother and reached for the milk jug. 'What did Mrs Tweedie want, Mum?' she asked, for something to say.

Rosemary sighed. 'Apparently she's got herself involved in the Spring Fair. She came to pick up the stuff we're giving to the secondhand clothes stall. She said the organisers were going to put prices on everything in the school assembly hall today. Luckily I had everything packed ready in that old laundry basket, so . . .'

Jessie went cold. The jug tipped sideways, and milk sloshed onto the table. She could hear her mother exclaiming, but she couldn't hear the words. Then she felt Rosemary taking the jug from her, and putting a cool hand on her forehead.

'Jessie, what's wrong? You're pale as a ghost!"

'I've—only got a bit of a headache,' Jessie managed to say. 'I'm all right.'

But she wasn't all right. There was a roaring in her ears. Her mind had gone numb. She was staring across the table at the back door—at the place where the basket of clothes had stood.

The basket had gone. And the Star Cloak had gone with it.

CHAPTER EIGHT

The Longest Day

essie could hardly remember the next twenty minutes. There were just flashes. Her mother looking worried, saying perhaps she wasn't well and should stay home from school. Her own desperate insistence that she was fine, and wanted to go—*had* to go. A blurred memory of a heart-wrenching run to school.

All the time her mind was filled with horrible pictures. Someone unpacking Mum's basket. Someone finding the black velvet bag, pulling out the Star Cloak, shaking out its glittering folds. The sunlight pouring through the long assembly hall windows. The Star Cloak crumpling, fading . . . turning into a limp, gray rag.

When she arrived at school, the playground was almost deserted, because she was so early. The parking lot was empty except for Ms Stone's small neat, dark green car and a yellow car she'd never seen before.

She sat down on a bench that overlooked the parking lot and waited. One by one teachers arrived, parked their cars, and went up to the school. Behind her she could hear the playground filling up. There was a lot of shouting and laughing. A group started playing handball. And still there was no sign of Mrs Tweedie.

The bell began to ring. It was time to go into class. Jessie sat where she was, gripping the rough wood of the bench.

'Better get a move on, Jessie!' Jessie jumped and spun around. Mr Thom was walking towards her, his white teeth flashing in a cheerful smile. He had a couple of boys with him. They were watching Jessie curiously.

Mr Thom turned to them. 'The car's parked behind the assembly hall,' he said. 'The lady's waiting for you. Her name's Mrs Tweedie. Carry everything into the hall storeroom, then come straight to class.'

The boys sped off. Jessie stared after them, feeling sick. She'd completely forgotten about the school's side entrance, behind the assembly hall. Those gates were usually locked. They were used only by people coming to fix things or . . . deliver things.

'Are you okay, Jess?' Mr Thom asked. 'Bell's rung, you know.'

Jessie swallowed. 'I—I have to see Mrs Tweedie,' she said. 'We gave her something by mistake. I've got to—'

'Right now, you've got to go to class,' said Mr Thom breezily. 'You can pop into the assembly hall at lunchtime. Off you go, now.' And he watched her all the way to her classroom to make sure she did as she was told.

Never had Jessie gone to class so unwillingly. As she sidled through the door and went to sit in her usual place beside Sal, Ms Stone glanced at her, but went on speaking.

'. . . and as you may have heard, Petra Connelly is in the assembly hall, reading the entries for the story competition,' she said. She waited for the class's excited murmuring to die down, then went on. 'She'll be there all day, because there are rather a lot of entries. Unfortunately, the other local schools seem to have sent every story handed in to them, instead of choosing just a few.'

'I think that's fairer,' Sal whispered. 'Your story should have gone in the competition, Jessie, it really—' She fell silent as Ms Stone's icy blue gaze swept over her.

'Mrs Connelly has a lot of reading to do, and she is *not* to be disturbed,' Ms Stone went on. 'So the hall is closed to all students today. No excuses, no exceptions.'

The class groaned. Jessie's heart sank to the soles of her shoes. Obviously Mr Thom hadn't known about this. Slowly she put up her hand. 'I—I have to get something we sent to the clothes stall by mistake,' she said. 'The clothes are in the assembly hall storeroom. Can I—?'

'I said, "no excuses, no exceptions", Jessica,' said Ms Stone crisply. 'Your mother can ring one of the organisers tonight, and they'll put the item aside for her. Now, maths books out, please . . .'

The morning dragged by. Jessie sat in a miserable daze, completely unable to concentrate. At morning break, she hung around behind some bushes near the assembly hall, waiting for a chance to slip inside. But it was impossible. The back door was locked, and Ms Stone was keeping guard on the doors at the front. It was the same at lunchtime.

'Jessie, what's wrong?' Sal whispered when they met in the classroom after lunch. 'Why are you acting so weird?'

'Sal, could you see through the assembly hall windows from where you were?' Jessie asked urgently. 'Do you know if they've started going through the secondhand clothes yet?'

Sal stared at her. 'That's not till after school,' she said. 'Ellie Lew told me. Her mother's coming. Tina Barassi's mum, too, and Mrs Wells.'

Jessie felt weak with relief. 'I've got to get into the hall, Sal,' she blurted out. 'I've *got* to get something from the storeroom, whatever Ms Stone says.'

Sal's eyes widened, but she didn't ask any questions. That was the great thing about Sal. All she said was, 'Well, I'll help you, then. But you'll get into big trouble if you're caught.'

The last class of the day was choir practice with Mrs Klein. As soon as the bell rang signalling the end of school, Jessie and Sal grabbed their bags and ran to the assembly hall. But Ms Stone was there before them. She stood at the front doors, jingling a bunch of keys, keeping a sharp eye on the students streaming towards the school gates.

In minutes the playground was almost empty, but Ms Stone stayed where she was. From behind the shelter of the bushes, Jessie watched in dismay as Mrs Lew and Mrs Wells walked, chatting, up from the parking lot. Ms Stone gave them the keys and they strolled on, around to the back of the hall. The sorting of the secondhand clothes was about to start.

'Jessie!' Sal hissed in her ear. 'Go after Mrs Lew. She'll leave the back door open for sure because Mrs Barassi isn't here yet. I'll go and talk to old Stone-face, to make her look the other way. Then I'll have to go, or she'll get suspicious. Okay?'

Jessie nodded. 'Thanks, Sal,' she managed to say.

Sal grinned. 'Good luck!' she whispered, and slipped away. Jessie watched tensely as her friend reached Ms Stone and started talking, opening her bag and shaking her head as if she'd lost something. Sal pointed back towards the classroom, and Ms Stone turned with her.

Now! Jessie ran to the back of the hall. Just as Sal had said, the door was ajar. Jessie peeped inside. An empty corridor stretched ahead of her. She could hear voices echoing from the front of the hall.

Her heart pounding, Jessie crept into the corridor. It was lined with doors. All were shut except the last one on the left, which was propped open by a fat bag of clothes. The storeroom!

Jessie ran along the corridor on tiptoe and darted into the storeroom, almost falling over a clutter of boxes and bags heaped just inside the doorway. She couldn't see her mother's basket, but she knew it was there. She could feel the Star Cloak. Her skin had begun to prickle, and little thrills of excitement were running through her arms and legs.

She edged around the untidy heap, straining her eyes in the dimness, and at last saw her mother's old laundry basket, right at the back. Several bags of clothes had been piled on top of it. As quietly as she could, she pushed the bags aside and plunged her hand into the basket. She found the black velvet bag, pulled it out, forced it into her jacket pocket, and zipped the pocket up.

Now all I have to do is to get out of here without

being caught, Jessie thought. She crept to the storeroom doorway and peered out. The corridor was empty. Gripping her bulging pocket tightly, she began running for the back door.

She was almost there when, to her horror, she heard a bump from outside and the back door moved. Someone carrying a box was elbowing the door open. Jessie glimpsed the sleeve of a pale grey jacket, and a slim wrist with a silver watchband. Ms Stone!

Jessie's eyes fell on a closed door just ahead of her. She leaped forward and frantically twisted the knob, praying it wasn't locked. The knob turned. Jessie plunged through the door, shut it, and leaned against it, panting.

Only then did she realise that the room wasn't empty. A pleasant-looking woman with short grey hair and glasses sat behind a cluttered desk in the centre. The woman stared at Jessie, the pen in her hand poised in midair, her eyes wide with surprise.

Jessie took a breath to stammer an apology, then froze as there was a knock on the door. 'It's Lyn Stone,' Ms Stone's voice said crisply.

Jessie clapped her hand over her mouth to stifle a squeak of fear. The woman behind the desk regarded her with interest. Then she put a finger to her lips and made a small sideways gesture with her other hand.

Wondering, Jessie slid aside. The door swung open, hiding her from view. She flattened herself against the wall, a cold wall heater digging into her spine.

'Here are the rest of our school's entries, Mrs Connelly, for the display you suggested,' she heard Ms Stone say politely. 'I'll just put them with the others you've already read, to keep them together.'

Jessie's face began to burn. The woman behind the desk was Petra Connelly! What must she think? What was she going to do?

'Again, I must apologise for the number of entries the other schools sent,' Ms Stone said. 'You must be getting very tired.'

'Not at all,' Petra Connelly answered cheerily. 'In fact, for some reason I feel quite shivery with excitement at the moment. You're shivering, too, I see. Isn't that strange?'

They can feel the Star Cloak, Jessie thought, pressing her hands together in terror.

'It's just a little chilly in here,' Ms Stone said. 'I'll turn on the heater.'

'No!' Petra Connelly said quickly. 'I mean . . . just have a look at this story first. It's really very good!'

Jessie heard Ms Stone's footsteps move further into the room. She peeped around the edge of the door. Ms Stone was bending over the desk, reading a story written on pink paper. Petra Connelly was looking over Ms Stone's shoulder, straight at Jessie. As Jessie stared, Petra Connelly winked and jerked her head slightly.

The message was clear. Jessie edged out from behind the door and crept to the doorway. She mouthed 'thank you', then slipped out of the room. In seconds she had reached the back door and let herself out into the deserted playground. Expecting every moment to hear Ms Stone calling her name, she fled to the bushes, picked up her bag, and pounded toward the school gate.

Jogging home, she thought her terrible day was nearly over, but she was wrong. As she rounded the corner into her own street, she saw the car pulling out of Blue Moon, her mother at the wheel. The car came to an abrupt stop beside her.

'Jessie, where have you been?' Rosemary exclaimed, throwing open the passenger door. 'I was coming to find you. Get in! I managed to get an appointment at the hairdresser for you, but it's in forty minutes, and I have to do all the shopping first.'

Jessie found her voice. 'Mum, no!' she panted. 'I have to—I don't need a haircut.'

'Of course you do,' said Rosemary. 'It's all hanging in your eyes. That's probably what's giving you these headaches. Hurry up, now!'

I should just run, Jessie thought frantically. I should just run to the secret garden, disappear into the Realm, and explain later. That's what a kid in a film would do.

But this wasn't a film. This was real life, and Rosemary was waiting, tapping the wheel impatiently. Almost crying with frustration, Jessie got into the car.

CHAPTER NINE

Wish Night

hen at last Jessie and her mother got back to Blue Moon, the sun was going down. It was nearly time for Wish Night to begin.

Queen Helena must know the Cloak's missing by now, Jessie thought as she heaved bags of groceries out of the car and ran to the house. She'll be frantic! On Stardust Mountain, the workers will be getting ready to gather the stardust. And Flash and her warriors will be swarming out of the Cavern, hunting for poor Giff. Oh, I have to *hurry!*

Granny turned from the kitchen window to greet them as they came in. She looked rather pale, but the moment she laid eyes on Jessie's backpack, her green eyes flashed, and Jessie knew that she felt the Star Cloak's magic. Jessie's heart leaped. Granny would help her. Granny would—

'Two little friends of yours came while you were out, Jessie,' Granny said. 'They were very sorry to have missed you.'

Jessie's eyes widened. Granny was looking at her intently. Obviously the 'two little friends' were Maybelle and Patrice. In desperation they'd come to Granny for help. How astonished they must have been to hear that Jessie had been home all day!

Jessie began to edge towards the back door. 'They might still be hanging around,' she said. 'I'll just go and—'

'No!' Rosemary said firmly. 'I want you to go and lie down, Jessie. You've been miserable all afternoon. You might be getting the flu or something. I feel a bit shivery myself, actually.'

Jessie glanced at her grandmother for help, but to her surprise and dismay, Granny shook her head. 'It's too late to go into the garden now, Jessie,' she said. 'I saw the first star a minute ago. Very soon, the sky will be full of them. It's just too late.'

A painful lump rose in Jessie's throat. *Too late.*

Granny was telling her that she'd never get from the secret Door to the palace in time to save Wish Night, or Giff.

'My advice is to do what your mum says and go to your room for a while,' Granny said, slowly and clearly. 'You'll be able to see the first star from your window, and you can make a wish. That will make you feel better, won't it?'

Jessie's heart leaped as she understood what Granny was telling her. Of course! Why hadn't she thought of it herself? She nodded quickly and darted out of the kitchen.

In moments she was closing the door of her room behind her. The curtains were open to the darkening sky. She took the velvet bag from her backpack and gently pulled out the Star Cloak. It looked perfect. She couldn't even see where the ugly tear had been.

The Cloak whispered around her, cool and tingling, as she put it on. The strings tied easily, as if they were tying themselves. She ran to the window and looked out at the first star. 'I wish I was in the palace with Queen Helena,' she whispered, and cool, blue shadows closed in around her.

The next moment, three joyful voices were shrilling in her ears, and eager hands were helping her to her feet. She stood, swaying, as the Star Cloak was taken from her shoulders.

When at last her eyes came back into focus, she saw that she was in the great entrance hall of the palace. Patrice was clinging to her arm. Maybelle was on her other side, pawing the ground with excitement. And Queen Helena was standing before her, wearing a flowing dress of silver, a sparkling silver crown, and the Star Cloak, blue as the blue moon and shimmering with magic.

Except for the four of them, the entrance hall was empty. The great, golden front doors were closed.

'Am I in time?' Jessie managed to ask.

Queen Helena hugged her. It was like being hugged by moonlight that smelled of flowers. 'Just in time,' Helena whispered. 'I knew you'd do it somehow, Jessie. I never lost hope.'

'Neither did I, dearie,' said Patrice loyally.

'I did,' snorted Maybelle, shaking her mane. 'I've aged ten years in the last ten minutes. And where, may I ask, is that fool of an elf who caused all this?'

Jessie felt a stab of panic as she suddenly remembered. 'Giff's lost on Stardust Mountain,' she said urgently. 'The star fairy warriors are really angry with him. They're hunting him! We've got to help him. He's—'

'Later, we will talk,' Queen Helena said quickly. 'There is no time now.' She turned and held up her hand.

The golden doors swung open, revealing the broad palace steps and the huge crowd gathered on the ground below. Queen Helena walked out of the palace to stand smiling on the topmost step with the Star Cloak swirling around her. The crowd gave a mighty roar. Fairies, elves, gnomes, pixies, sprites, dwarfs, miniature horses, the tall beautiful people called the Folk, and hundreds of other magical beings Jessie had never seen before, were cheering as one.

But this was not what made Jessie gasp in awe. It was the sky—the sky ablaze with stars that were so huge, so bright, that the whole, vast canopy looked like a twinkling mass of silver and gold.

'Quickly!' snapped Maybelle. 'Outside, or we'll miss out on the wishes!'

The wishes, Jessie thought. Of course! I can wish, too. I can have anything I want—anything that's possible, Giff said. But here in the Realm, almost anything's possible. Almost anything . . .

No one noticed Jessie, Patrice and Maybelle

slip silently through the doorway, and hurry down one side of the stairs. The crowd had eyes only for their Queen.

The Star Cloak swirled and glittered. Queen Helena raised her arms to the sky. Everyone looked up. The stars above them seemed to lean closer. Then, with a strange, beautiful sound, like sighing music, stars began to fall, swooping downward like enormous birds, their trailing tails of silver light making swirling patterns in the sky. Jessie watched, transfixed. Her ears were filled with the music of the falling stars. She was shivering all over.

'Now,' she heard Patrice whisper. 'Remember, Jessie. Wish for the thing you want most. The dearest wish of your heart.'

The sky music rose. One of the stars burst in a shower of sparks. Then another did the same, and another. The sky was filled with blazing light. The crowd cried out as glittering stardust began to fall like rain.

Then there was silence, except for the singing of the stars, and Jessie knew that all around her people were wishing.

. . . *the thing you want most. The dearest wish of your heart.*

There were so many things she could wish for. But as the stardust settled on her face and hands, and spangled her hair, she knew that there was only one thing that really mattered. She shut her eyes and wished, with all her heart, for Giff to come home.

She repeated her wish many times. Then she realised that the star music had died away. Slowly she opened her eyes again. The falling stars had gone. The air around her was filled with glittering specks of light. Everywhere fairy folk were dancing and clapping, while above them arched the canopy of the sky, black velvet sprinkled with tiny diamonds.

Jessie looked around quickly. Maybelle's mane and tail were frosted with starlight. Patrice's face was glowing. But there was no sign of Giff. The lump rose in Jessie's throat again. She had so hoped . . .

'What's the matter, dearie?' Patrice asked anxiously. 'Surely you didn't forget to wish?'

'No. But . . . but my wish hasn't come true,' Jessie whispered, fighting back her tears.

Maybelle whisked her tail, showering Patrice with more stardust. 'You can't expect miracles, you know,' she said. 'I mean, things don't just appear out of thin air just because you wish for them. That's not how it works. You often have to wait—for quite a long time, sometimes. And you never know exactly how it's going to happen. Giff wished for the Star Cloak to be mended, didn't he? In the end it was—but not in the way he meant.'

'Once, Giff wished for his hair to turn blue,' Patrice giggled. 'He was really disappointed when it didn't. Then, a couple of months later, he fell into a tub of blue rainbow crystals in the storehouse.'

'His hair turned blue then, all right!' Maybelle snorted. 'So did the rest of him. He was completely blue for days. What a sight he was!'

She and Patrice laughed, and even Jessie smiled. But the laughter died away quickly. Maybelle cleared her throat uncomfortably, and Patrice's round face grew troubled. Jessie knew they were both wondering if they would ever see their friend again.

She couldn't bear it. Quickly she turned away and looked up at the sky. It was hard to believe that only minutes ago it had been exploding with silver light. It looked completely normal now. At least . . .

Jessie frowned, and shook her head. For a moment it had looked as if some of the new stars were moving. My eyes are playing tricks on me, she thought. But when she looked again, she saw exactly what she had seen before. Hundreds of stars, packed tightly together, were speeding towards the palace.

CHAPTER TEN

Surprises

'atrice, Maybelle, look!' Jessie gasped. 'More stars are falling.'

'Oh no, Jessie, that's all over,' murmured Patrice. 'There are only new stars in the sky now, and they— Oh!'

'What in the Realm . . . ?' said Maybelle, at the same moment.

They had both looked up at last. They had seen the glittering mass shooting towards them. Others in the crowd had seen it, too. Everywhere there were shouts of surprise and alarm.

'What's happening?' squeaked Patrice.

'I don't know,' muttered Maybelle, pawing the

ground nervously. 'I've never heard of new stars acting like this. They're coming at us very fast, too. I think we should—'

But Patrice and Jessie never found out what Maybelle thought they should do. Because at that very moment the mass of light streaked down from the sky like a huge, humming arrow, and something crashed to the ground between them, knocking them all sprawling.

Everyone was screaming. Her head spinning, her ears ringing, Jessie crawled to her knees, trying to understand what had happened. She saw the arrow of light speeding away across the sky. She saw the milling crowd of fairy folk parting to make way as Queen Helena came running. She saw Patrice and Maybelle lying gasping on the ground, all the breath knocked out of them. And right beside her, whimpering, scratched, bedraggled, and covered in mud, was . . .

'Giff!' Jessie squealed. She threw her arms around the elf, and hugged him tight. 'Oh, Giff, you're home! My wish came true!'

'*Your* wish?' cried Patrice. 'Goodness, Jessie, that was *my* wish, too.'

'And mine,' Maybelle admitted gruffly. 'I was going to wish for a nice, juicy patch of four-leafed clover, but I missed Giff, for some reason, so I wished for him instead. I must have been out of my mind.'

Patrice laughed. 'No wonder you arrived in such a rush, Giff,' she said. 'Three wishes, all for you!'

'Four, actually,' said a gentle voice. 'I wished for Giff to come home, too.' Everyone looked up and saw Queen Helena smiling down at them. Patrice, Maybelle and Jessie scrambled to their feet. Giff moaned, and covered his muddy face with his hands.

'Oh dear, oh dear,' he wailed. 'You all wasted your wishes on me! And I'm not worth it! I'm so sorry I tore the Star Cloak, Queen Helena! I'm so sorry I ran away! I'm so sorry I put Jessie in danger! I was just so scared when Loris and the guards came after me—'

'Giff!' Queen Helena shook her head and bent to pull the little elf to his feet. 'Last night, I didn't even know the Star Cloak was missing! The guards were only trying to find you because the griffins were causing trouble, and you had the last box of griffin treats.'

Giff's jaw dropped. He felt inside his jacket and pulled out a very crumpled yellow box decorated with a picture of a smiling griffin. 'Oh,' he said weakly. 'I forgot.'

'I don't believe it!' groaned Maybelle.

'Oh, leave him alone,' said Patrice. 'He's been punished enough.'

'I agree,' Queen Helena said quietly. 'But from now on, Giff, come and *tell* me if something bad happens, even if it's your fault. If you'd done that last night, I could have taken the Cloak to Stardust Mountain myself, and you and Jessie and all of us would have been saved a lot of worry and trouble.'

'Yes, Giff. It's very lucky that when the star fairy warriors found you, they agreed to bring you home,' Patrice put in. 'They could have hurt you very badly.'

'One of them nearly did,' snuffled Giff. 'Her name was Flash, and she was really fierce. But another one called Gleam stopped her. Gleam said that Jessie had forgiven Flash for attacking her, so Flash should forgive *me* for damaging the Star Cloak. Gleam said that would make Jessie glad, and pay back what Flash owed her.'

He wiped his eyes with the back of his hand and sniffed again. 'Gleam talked and talked and finally the others agreed—even Flash. And they were just about to go away and leave me in the awful, muddy hole they found me in, when the stars started falling. Then all of them suddenly got really happy and excited, and somehow they got the idea to carry me home.'

'Thanks to our wishes,' Maybelle said sourly.

'Only the coming-home part,' Patrice said, putting her arm around Giff. 'The coming-home-*safe* part was all thanks to Jessie.'

<hr />

'You look *so* much better this morning, Jessie,' Rosemary said, at breakfast. 'You must have had a good night.'

'Oh, I *did*.' Jessie sighed. It was true, though she was sure that feasting and celebrating till midnight in the Realm wasn't the sort of 'good night' her mother meant.

She went to the Spring Fair feeling as if a huge weight had rolled off her shoulders. When the time came, she stood on the assembly hall stage with the rest of the choir, and sang with real joy. But when Petra Connelly came on stage with Ms Stone to announce the winners of the story competition, Jessie felt herself beginning to blush, and edged a little behind Sal. The thought of the narrow escape she'd had in the hall yesterday still made her stomach turn over.

Ms Stone made a speech welcoming Petra Connelly. Then Petra Connelly spoke about the high standard of the stories and said how much she'd enjoyed the judging. Then she said it was time to announce the winner. And she called Jessie's name.

For a moment, Jessie didn't move. She was sure that she'd imagined it.

'Jessie!' hissed Sal, nudging her violently. 'Jessie, it's you! Go on!'

Astounded, Jessie stumbled from her place and walked to the front of the stage. Everyone was clapping, especially the choir. When Petra Connelly saw Jessie, her eyes widened in surprise, then she beamed.

'Well, well,' she murmured, shaking Jessie's hand and giving her the big parcel of books that was the competition's first prize. 'So we meet again.'

'I . . . I think there's been a mistake,' Jessie stammered, knowing her face must be bright red. 'My story wasn't one of the finalists. It was about— about a unicorn.' She glanced over her shoulder. Ms Stone's face was rigid.

'That's the one!' exclaimed Petra Connelly, in a louder voice, so that Ms Stone, and the whole audience, could hear her. 'The unicorn story. Wonderful! It was in the box of entries Ms Stone brought in after school.'

'Yes,' said Ms Stone, through tight lips.

'You see,' said Petra Connelly, her smile broadening, 'I felt so full of energy after . . . after your visit, Ms Stone, that I decided to look at all the entries in that box, as well as the others I had. Why not? I thought. You never know. And, after all, I am the judge.'

She smiled at Ms Stone, completely ignoring her obvious annoyance. 'And as soon as I read the unicorn story, I knew I had my winner,' she went on. 'It was about fantastic things, of course, but while I was reading it, I really believed it. You believed it, too, while you were writing it, didn't you, Jessica?'

'Oh, yes,' Jessie said. 'Completely!'

'And that's the sign of a real writer,' said Petra Connelly. 'Keep it up!'

Then everyone clapped again, and Ms Stone had no choice but to make her speech of thanks and watch Petra Connelly being presented with a bunch of flowers, just as if she wasn't furious but felt absolutely fine.

'Old Stone-face must be so angry,' Sal giggled as she and Jessie left the hall after it was all over. 'I hope she doesn't pick on you even more now.'

Jessie shook her head. She knew that in a way Ms Stone was like the star fairy warriors. She was cold, but she was fair. She wouldn't allow herself the weakness of showing her feelings. And her logical mind would tell her that the whole thing had been Petra Connelly's fault, not Jessie's.

But Jessie was sure that if it hadn't been for the Star Cloak, and that restless, excited feeling it gave everyone around it, Petra Connelly would never have opened the box Ms Stone brought to her room. Then she would never have read the unicorn story.

So really I won the competition because the Star Cloak was lost, Jessie thought. It's so strange. But Ms Stone doesn't know about the Star Cloak. And even if I told her about it, she wouldn't believe me. Poor Ms Stone.

'So,' Sal was saying with satisfaction. 'Everything worked out really well in the end, didn't it?'

'Yes,' Jessie said. 'It did.'

She thought of the star fairies, sleeping

contentedly after their long night's work. She thought of Giff, safe at home again. She thought of the Star Cloak, back in the Realm treasure house for another year. She thought of the tiny gold star that Queen Helena had fastened to her charm bracelet before wishing her home. She thought of what her mother would say, when she heard about the prize.

And smiling, she walked with Sal out into the sun.

A charm bracelet opens
a magical world of adventure

The Peskie Spell

EMILY RODDA

CHAPTER ONE

Pesky Weather

It was a fine, sunny Sunday, but a wild wind blew around the old house called Blue Moon, rattling the windows and tossing the branches of the trees. Red and yellow leaves swirled in the air like flocks of small, bright birds.

Inside the house, Jessie glanced up at the leaves flying past the high windows of her grandfather's studio. She felt jumpy and uneasy. She was supposed to be dusting a pile of sketchbooks she'd taken from a glass-fronted cabinet, but she just couldn't concentrate.

'This is what Granny calls "pesky weather,"' she said to her mother, who was sweeping the studio floor. 'Remember that song she always sings when it's sunny and windy both at the same time?'

Rosemary smiled and began to sing, moving her broom in time to the music:

'Pesky weather, nothing goes right!
Pesky weather, lock the Doors tight!
Make a magic brew
With seven drops of dew,
A drop of thistle milk,
And a strand of spider silk . . .'

She broke off, laughing. 'Well, things have gone right for us today, Jess, in spite of the pesky weather,' she said. 'The studio's looking pretty good, now. It'll just need a quick dust before the photographer comes on Thursday.'

'Will Granny be home by then?' Jessie asked. Her grandmother was away seeing some people at the National Gallery who were organising a big exhibition of her late husband's famous fairy paintings. The exhibition was to be held in a few months' time, and a photograph of the Blue Moon studio was going to be part of it.

'Oh, yes,' Rosemary said. 'She'll be back on Tuesday night. How are you going with those sketchbooks, Jess?'

'Nearly finished,' said Jessie hastily. She knew she'd been spending more time looking at the books than cleaning them. The one she was holding now was filled with sketches of trees, leaves, and flowers, and she'd found some real flowers pressed between the pages, too—forget-me-nots, violets, and many other flowers she didn't know.

'Can I borrow this one, Mum?' she asked, holding up the book.

'Sure,' her mother said. 'Just be careful with it. And don't take it outside.'

Jessie put the sketchbook on top of the glass-fronted cabinet and went on dusting the other books and stacking them away.

It was her grandfather's fairy paintings that had made him famous, but he'd painted landscapes, trees, flowers, birds, and animals, too. People who saw his sketchbooks were always fascinated. 'What an imagination Robert Belairs had,' they'd say. 'It's just as if fantasy creatures like griffins and mermaids were just as real to him as lizards and cockatoos!'

Little did they know that there was a very good reason for this—the best reason in the world. Jessie's grandfather had seen griffins and mermaids and other strange beings with his own eyes. He'd seen them in the magical world of the Realm, after he discovered an invisible Door at the bottom of the Blue Moon garden. For years he'd brought back sketches from the Realm. Then, one day, he'd brought back something else: the Realm princess called Jessica, who was to become his wife, Rosemary's mother, and Jessie's very special grandmother.

Only Jessie shared Granny's secret. She'd discovered it by accident and had promised to keep it. She knew she couldn't tell anyone about the Realm. But how she'd have loved to talk about it with her mother, with her best friend, Sal—and even with her school teacher, Ms Stone, who was always criticising her for writing about magical things instead of what Ms Stone called 'real life'!

If only she could tell them about the Realm— and about her friends Giff the elf, Maybelle the miniature horse, Patrice the palace housekeeper, and Queen Helena, who ruled the Realm in her sister Jessica's place! If only she could tell them that every charm on the gold bracelet now jingling softly on her wrist was a gift from the Realm to remind her of an exciting adventure.

The Realm . . .

Jessie frowned. Thoughts of the Realm had brought back the restless, uneasy feeling and now it was stronger than ever.

'Jessie, is something wrong?'

Jessie looked up quickly, meeting her mother's puzzled eyes. 'You've obviously got something on your mind,' Rosemary said. 'Is Ms Stone giving you trouble at school again?'

Jessie forced a smile. 'No,' she said. 'Ms Stone's concentrating on Lisa Wells and Rachel Lew at the moment. She followed them up from the car park on Friday morning and saw that they were jumping over all the cracks in the path. When she asked them why, they said it was because stepping on a crack was bad luck.' Despite herself, she giggled.

Rosemary laughed with her. 'I can just imagine what Ms Stone said about *that*!' she said, turning back to her sweeping.

'Yeah,' said Jessie. 'In class she went on for ages about how stupid it was to believe in things like that. Then she asked everyone to tell her all the sayings about bad luck they knew. She wrote them down and said that on Monday she was going to prove that none of them is true.'

Rosemary shook her head. 'Your Ms Stone's really got a bee in her bonnet about make-believe, hasn't she?' she said. 'It's as if she's on a one-woman quest to stamp it out. She's right about superstitions being silly, of course. But she won't be able to *prove* it. In fact—'

'Yoo-hoo!' called a voice from the back door. 'It's only me.'

Jessie and her mother exchanged rueful glances. 'Come in, Louise,' Rosemary called back. 'We're in the studio.'

Mrs Tweedie, their next-door neighbour, appeared at the studio door. Her spiky grey hair had been blown about by the wind, and her pointed nose was bright red at the tip. Flynn, Granny's big orange cat, was stalking behind her, looking very disapproving.

'I won't disturb you,' said Mrs Tweedie, bustling into the room. 'I just popped in to bring you a few fruit slices I made this morning. They're on the kitchen table.'

'Oh—thank you, Louise,' Rosemary said. 'You are kind.'

It's just an excuse to come in here and poke around, Jessie thought crossly. Then she felt a bit mean. Obviously Mrs Tweedie was lonely. She was avid for details about other peoples' lives because she didn't have any life of her own.

Mrs Tweedie began wandering around the studio, her sharp, bird-like eyes darting everywhere. 'Have you heard from your mother today yet, Rosemary?'

she asked, stopping at the glass-fronted cabinet and beginning to leaf through the sketchbook lying there.

'We won't be hearing from her again till Tuesday,' said Rosemary. 'Her next meeting isn't till then, so she's gone off on a bird-watching camp with some group she met at the gallery.'

'*Really?*' gushed Mrs Tweedie. 'Oh, isn't she *marvellous.*'

'Marvellous,' Rosemary agreed dryly. 'But I wish she'd agree to get a mobile phone. Well, Louise, we'd better—'

'Oh!' squealed Mrs Tweedie, bending over the sketchbook. 'Oh, look what I've found! A pressed flower—*perfectly* preserved! I even caught a whiff of its scent as I turned the page. Jessie, look at this!'

Jessie bit her tongue to stop herself saying that the sketchbook had *dozens* of pressed flowers in it, and that there was no need for Mrs Tweedie to make such a fuss.

But her irritation was replaced by sheer panic when she saw what Mrs Tweedie was looking at. The flower was as delicate as if it were made of fairy wings. Despite its age, its centre was still bright yellow and its petals were a beautiful blue.

Jessie knew without doubt that this was a flower

from the Realm. She'd never seen it before, but there was something about it that breathed magic. How like her grandfather to have put it in the book with perfectly ordinary flowers from the Blue Moon garden! And what bad luck that Mrs Tweedie had seen it!

'What sort of flower do you think it is?' Mrs Tweedie twittered. 'It's *most* unusual.'

'It's just a blue daisy, isn't it?' said Jessie, trying to keep her voice even.

'Oh, I don't think so,' said Mrs Tweedie, putting her head on one side. She whirled around to Rosemary and clasped her hands. 'I know it's a lot to ask,' she said breathlessly, 'but could I borrow this flower for a teeny while? I'd love to try to identify it.'

Jessie held her breath, then felt a wave of relief as her mother looked embarrassed and shook her head. 'I'm awfully sorry, Louise,' Rosemary said, 'but Dad's sketchbooks and all their contents, are—well, rather precious. I don't think it would be right to let anything leave the house—at least while Mum's away. I hope you understand.'

Mrs Tweedie flushed slightly. 'Oh—of course!' she said in rather a high voice. 'Of course. Well. I'd better be going. Don't bother to see me out. I know my way.'

She waved clumsily and hurried from the room. Flynn got up and padded after her, as if he was seeing her off the premises.

'Oh dear! Now I've hurt her feelings,' Rosemary said as the back door slammed.

'You were perfectly right, Mum!' said Jessie vehemently.

Rosemary smiled and shrugged. 'Look, I'll finish up here, Jessie,' she said. 'You go on outside. I know you're dying to get out into the pesky weather, and the fresh air might do you good. Just be indoors by sunset. All right?'

'All right!' Jessie promised gladly.

She took the sketchbook to her room. She pulled on a jacket, and was just about to rush out again when she thought of something. She grabbed an old grey cloak from the top of her wardrobe and stuffed it into her school backpack.

A minute later she was outside, the pack on her back, her long red hair whipping in the wind. She glanced over her shoulder to make sure that Mrs Tweedie wasn't watching over the fence, then ran for the secret garden.

Soon I'll be in the Realm, she thought. Then I'll know. Then I'll know . . .

In the secret garden, the rosemary bushes that

edged the little square of green lawn were as fragrant as ever. The high, clipped hedge still seemed to keep the whole world out.

Jessie gave a sigh of relief. 'Open!' she said. She closed her eyes and waited for the familiar cool, tingling breeze that always swept over her as she moved into the Realm.

But she didn't feel anything at all. And when she opened her eyes she found that nothing had changed. She was still in the secret garden. Jessie blinked in shock.

'Open!' she repeated unsteadily. But again nothing happened. The magic hadn't worked. The Door to the Realm hadn't opened.

She was locked out.

CHAPTER TWO

Maybelle to the Rescue

essie heard a soft, trilling sound behind her and turned quickly. Flynn was sitting in the entrance to the secret garden, watching her gravely.

'The Door's locked, Flynn,' Jessie said. 'Something awful is happening in the Realm, I know it! Oh, if only I could talk to Granny! But she's off bird watching or something, and I can't even ring her!'

She shook her head. 'I've been able to help the Realm before. Maybe I could help this time. But now I can't even try if I can't get in!'

Flynn stood up and stretched. Then he turned around and began walking away, his tail held high.

After a moment, he looked over his shoulder at Jessie. Clearly he expected her to follow him.

Wondering what was in his mind, Jessie let him lead her back up to the house and into the kitchen. To her surprise he didn't stop there, but moved on, into the hallway beyond.

'Where are you going?' Jessie called. But Flynn didn't stop. She hurried after him, and was just in time to see him disappearing into her grandmother's bedroom. Very puzzled now, she followed him.

She found him sitting below the painting that hung on the wall facing Granny's bed. He turned his head toward her and miaowed.

Jessie's eyes widened as she stared at the picture on the wall. Dim and mysterious looking, it showed an archway in a high green hedge, with a blue moon floating in the sky above.

'The secret Door!' Jessie whispered. 'But, Flynn . . . this is Granny's special, private way into the Realm. Do you really think I should—?'

Flynn yawned. It was exactly as if he were saying, 'Do you want to get into the Realm or not?'

Jessie took a deep breath. She moved farther into the room and stood directly in front of the painting. 'Open!' she said in a loud, clear voice.

There was a rush of cold wind. The archway in the painting grew larger and larger, till it was all Jessie could see. She could feel her hair flying around her head. Her skin began to tingle. The sound of wind filled her ears. She screwed her eyes shut as she felt herself being swept away.

After a dizzying moment, she felt soft earth beneath her feet. She waited breathlessly for the wind to die down, for the familiar, sweet sounds of the Realm to reach her ears.

But it didn't happen. The sound of the wind went on and on, mingled with a shrill, chirruping sound that seemed to go right through Jessie's head. And now her skin wasn't just tingling. It was itching unbearably.

What's happening? Jessie thought in confusion. She forced her eyes open and blinked in the bright sunlight.

She was in the Realm. She was standing in front of Queen Helena's palace, on the broad swathe of grass where the Realm folk often gathered.

But nothing looked as it usually did. The trees were tossing in the wind. There were no elves, no fairies, no miniature horses, or palace guards to be seen. The air was thick with whirling shapes that looked like small green leaves. The trembling grass was littered with odd shoes, squashed hats, torn handkerchiefs, and tangled ribbons.

Jessie rubbed her streaming eyes. And then she saw that the green things swirling around her weren't leaves, as she had first thought, but masses of small, flying creatures.

The creatures had hard little wings, thin springy legs, and wild, mischievous, pointed faces like upside-down triangles. Chirruping and clicking, they swooped around Jessie's head, their tiny eyes sparkling like shiny black beads. They were everywhere. The grass and the trees were thick with them. They were swarming all over the palace steps. They were . . .

Jessie screamed as she realised the creatures were swarming all over her, too. Hundreds of them were tickling her, pinching her and tugging at her hair, her clothes and her shoes.

Frantically she tried to brush them off, but it was impossible. Clicking and giggling, the creatures tumbled away under her hands, then darted back instantly to begin their teasing all over again.

Jessie tried to run, and almost at once she tripped and fell. The little green creatures had untied her shoelaces. Gasping, she scrambled to her feet. Then, with a stab of joy, she heard a familiar voice calling her name. She looked up and saw Maybelle galloping toward her through a swirling green cloud. Frayed ribbons hung loose and flapping in Maybelle's tangled mane. Her eyes were wild.

'Maybelle!' Jessie screamed at the top of her voice.

'Jessie, what are you *doing* here?' roared Maybelle, racing up to her. 'No, don't tell me! Let's get out of this! Hold on to me.'

Jessie clutched her friend's mane. Green creatures wriggled out from under her fingers and began bouncing up and down on her hand, flapping their hard little wings and chirruping gleefully.

'Ignore them!' ordered Maybelle. 'Put your head down!'

She began trotting toward the palace. Holding on tightly, her head bent low, Jessie jogged beside her. After a moment the little horse veered to the right and began moving along the side of the palace, toward Patrice's apartment.

As they reached Patrice's door, Jessie noticed a strong smell of oranges. Before she had time to wonder about this, the green creatures clinging to her hands and feet began to squeak and fly away, wrinkling their tiny noses in disgust.

Maybelle kicked the door sharply. 'Patrice!' she bellowed. 'Open up! I've got her!'

There was a scuffling sound behind the door. Maybelle began shaking herself violently. Dozens of green creatures that had been hiding in her mane flew off with a chorus of indignant clicks. 'Brush yourself off, Jessie!' Maybelle shouted. 'Shake your head. Then as soon as the door opens, get in. Fast!'

The door swung open and Jessie bolted through it, with Maybelle hard on her heels. Patrice was waiting for them in her narrow hallway, a large jug of orange juice clutched in her hand. The moment they were safely inside, she slammed the door and stuffed the crack beneath it with an old rug. Then she whirled around to face them.

'Oh, Jessie!' she panted, clutching Jessie's arm. 'How in the Realm did you get here? Oh, what a shock I got when I heard your voice!'

She bustled Jessie into the kitchen, which was filled with the delicious smell of baking. She put the jug of orange juice on the table and pulled out a chair so that Jessie could sit down. 'And I never *would* have heard it, if I hadn't been sprinkling the doormat just at that very moment,' she chattered on. 'Orange juice helps keep them off, you know. For a while. Oh, Jessie, your poor hair—'

'*Her* hair?' Maybelle snorted. 'What about mine? Look at my mane! I'll never get the knots out!'

'Yes, you will,' Patrice said soothingly, bending to peep into the oven. 'I'll help you. But in the meantime, these honey snaps are almost ready. I'll get you both a nice, cool drink, and then—'

'Patrice! Maybelle! What's happening?' Jessie broke in desperately. 'What are those green things?'

'Peskies,' said Maybelle in tones of great disgust. 'They came down from the hills with the wind yesterday, and life's been impossible ever since.'

'*Peskies?*' Jessie gasped, her grandmother's little song suddenly taking on a whole new meaning.

'Here you are, dearie,' said Patrice, giving Jessie a tall glass of lemon drink. 'Just watch out for pips. I've strained it twice, but you never know with Peskies about.'

She put a bowl of lemon drink in front of Maybelle. Then, seeing that Jessie still looked bewildered, she poured a drink for herself and sat down at the table.

'You see, dearie, Peskies mean mischief,' she explained. 'When there are Peskies about, everything that *can* go wrong *does* go wrong. Buttons fall off. Shoelaces break. Things get lost. Milk boils over.

Plates and cups smash. Folk and creatures slip and fall . . .'

'Hair tangles,' grumbled Maybelle. 'Ribbons come loose—'

'Clocks stop,' said Patrice. 'Doorknobs fall off. Chairs collapse. Windows stick. Oh, Jessie, I just can't *begin* to tell you all the trouble Peskies cause.'

'But—there aren't any Peskies in here, are there?' asked Jessie, looking around nervously.

'There could be a few,' Patrice said. 'I've done my best to get rid of them, but they hide, the little wretches. Drink up, Jessie. It will do you good.'

Jessie took a cautious sip of her drink. It was deliciously cool. She began to feel a little better.

'And that's not the worst of it,' Maybelle said soberly. 'Peskies make mischief. But they also eat magic.'

'Eat magic?' Jessie gasped, horrified.

Maybelle nodded. 'They gobble it up,' she said. 'The longer they stay, and the more of them they are, the less magic there is. If we can't stop the plague soon—within a couple of days, I'd say—there'll be no magic left.'

'But can't Queen Helena—?' Jessie began desperately.

She was interrupted by a thunderous knocking at the door and the sound of muffled shrieking.

Patrice leaped to her feet and seized the jug of orange juice. 'Oh, no!' she cried. 'He *hasn't*! He *wouldn't*!'

She rushed out of the kitchen, juice slopping from the jug as she ran. Jessie jumped up and ran after her. She reached the hallway just in time to see Giff the elf tumbling through the front door waving an inside-out green umbrella at the mass of chirruping Peskies swarming in after him.

CHAPTER THREE

A Matter of Memory

'Get out, you little wretches!' screamed Patrice, splashing orange juice at the Peskies. 'Get out!'

The Peskies squeaked and scattered. Most flew out of the door again, but some darted into hiding, so fast that Jessie couldn't see where they had gone. Giff tried to run for the kitchen, slipped on a puddle of orange juice, and fell flat on the floor, wailing miserably.

Jessie ran to help him up. She'd only taken two steps when she felt her own feet sliding out from under her. Screaming, she fell on top of Giff. Patrice slammed the door, whirled around, slipped, and fell over them both. The jug flew high into the air, turning over and over. Orange juice fell like rain.

'Oh, no!' Patrice squealed. She watched in helpless fury as the jug emptied itself and then fell, landing neatly upside down on Giff's head.

'Help!' howled Giff, his voice strangely hollow and echoing. 'Help!' He began struggling wildly. Jessie and Patrice fought to untangle themselves, and at last managed to struggle to their feet. Together they seized the jug and pulled. It came off Giff's head with a loud *pop*, and they all fell backward again.

Watching them from her place of safety by the kitchen door, Maybelle sighed. Then her nose twitched and she looked over her shoulder.

'There's smoke coming out of the oven, Patrice,' she remarked.

'What!' shrieked Patrice. She crawled up and, with Jessie and Giff close behind her, staggered into the kitchen. She hobbled to the stove and tore the oven door open. Black smoke billowed out. Coughing and spluttering, Patrice seized a towel and used it to pull out a tray of what looked like flat, smoking pieces of coal.

'Oh, no!' wailed Giff. 'The honey snaps! They're ruined!'

Patrice dumped the tray into the sink and turned

on the tap. The tray hissed, and more smoke billowed upward. She turned to face her guests. Her hair was dripping with orange juice. Her apron was filthy. She looked furious.

'Giff!' she said in a quiet, dangerous voice. 'Why did you leave your tree house? What *possessed* you to go wandering around in—?'

'I wasn't wandering!' Giff protested, wringing his hands. 'I was coming here, for honey snaps! You said you were going to make some today, Patrice. And I was starving!'

Maybelle snorted. Giff nodded violently.

'I was *starving*!' he exclaimed. 'Last night, I was having a little snack before I went to bed. A Peskie pulled my hair and made me fall off my stool. I fell so hard that I made a hole in the floor. The cookie jar rolled through the hole and fell down to the ground. The cookies all spilled out, and a griffin ate every single one!'

He burst into tears, just thinking about it. Jessie put her arm around him, but Maybelle snorted again.

'You may not have had cookies, but you were *not* starving, Giff!' Patrice said, still in that frighteningly calm voice. 'You had bread and cheese, didn't you? You had fairy-apples. You had—'

'Well—yes.' Giff sobbed. 'But there are some times

when only a cookie will do, Patrice. And all today I just kept thinking, honey snaps, honey snaps, honey snaps, till I just couldn't stand it anymore! So I got out my umbrella, and—'

'*That* umbrella, I presume,' said Maybelle, nodding at the sad mess of spokes and tattered green silk still trailing from Giff's hand. 'Your *new* umbrella. The one *we* gave you for your birthday.'

Giff buried his face in his hands and howled.

'Oh, leave him alone, Maybelle.' Patrice sighed, her anger suddenly dying. 'Giff, it's all right. Stop crying, and I'll see if I can find something nice in the pantry.'

Giff brightened up very quickly at the mention of food. Patrice found a few chocolate chip cookies in a tin, and the four friends gathered around the kitchen table to share them.

'You still haven't told us how you got here, Jessie,' said Maybelle, with her mouth full. 'The first thing Queen Helena did when the Peskie plague started was to lock the Doors. We didn't have time to warn you—it had to be done quickly. Imagine what would happen if Peskies got into your world!'

'I think they do, sometimes,' Jessie said, remembering days at home and at school when nothing seemed to go right.

'Oh, you might have a few, now and then, just like us,' said Patrice. 'But this is different, Jessie. This is a real plague.'

Jessie nodded thoughtfully. 'I came by Granny's secret Door,' she said. 'She's away, but I was worried about you.'

Giff rubbed his cheek against her arm. 'We'll be all right now you're here, Jessie,' he said. 'You'll stop the Peskie plague, I know you will.'

Jessie bit her lip. She didn't see how. 'Can't Queen Helena do anything?' she asked.

Patrice frowned. 'The problem is, Peskies eat magic, so they're very strong. Ordinary banishing spells don't work on them. And it's been so long since the Realm had a Peskie plague that no one knows what to do about it—even Queen Helena. For hundreds of years, a squirt of orange juice has been enough to scare off the few Peskies who were a problem. This plague is another thing altogether.'

'But—but how did it happen?' Jessie stammered. 'I mean—why did the plague start?'

'No one knows,' said Giff. 'It just—happened!'

'Queen Helena is sure there used to be a spell that got rid of Peskies in the old days,' Maybelle put in. 'Not just words—but some sort of brew you made as well.'

'Helena thinks her mother knew it,' Patrice put in. 'She has an idea that there was a rhyme that gave all the ingredients for the brew. But she couldn't find it in the library anywhere.'

Jessie caught her breath. Suddenly her mind was filled with Granny's voice—singing . . .

'Now Helena's gone to see the Furrybears of Brill,' Maybelle was saying. 'The Furrybears know a million old stories. Helena's hoping that the Peskie rhyme might be repeated in one of them. It can't have just disappeared completely.'

'It hasn't!' Jessie heard herself saying, her voice high with excitement. 'It's in the words of an old song Granny sings!'

As her friends listened breathlessly, she began to sing:

'Pesky weather, nothing goes right!
Pesky weather, lock the Doors tight!
Make a magic brew
With seven drops of dew,
A drop of thistle milk,
And a strand of spider silk . . .'

She trailed off, unable to think what came next. 'Try again,' Maybelle urged.

Jessie sang the words again. She could feel the others holding their breath, willing her to go on. But again she stopped. The next line just would not come. She buried her face in her hands.

'You're trying too hard,' said Patrice. 'Just relax for a minute.'

'Are there any more cookies?' Giff asked, looking longingly at the empty plate in front of him.

'No,' Patrice said shortly. 'Make yourself some bread and honey, if you're hungry.'

'You're asking for trouble, Patrice,' muttered Maybelle as Giff scurried eagerly to the pantry. 'There are Peskies about. You've already got orange juice all over the floor. Honey on the ceiling will be the next thing.'

'Oh!' squealed Jessie. She leaped up and her chair tipped backward and fell to the floor with a crash. Maybelle and Patrice jumped. Giff, who was just coming out from the pantry with his arms full, threw up his hands in shock. A loaf of bread and a pot of honey sailed through the air.

'N-o-o!' howled Patrice. Desperately she threw herself forward and caught the honey pot just before it hit the table.

'Good catch!' said Maybelle, then yelled as the loaf of bread hit her on the head and broke in half, covering her with crumbs.

The Peskies who had been hiding under the pantry door giggled wickedly.

'I've got it!' Jessie cried, as if none of this was happening at all. 'Maybelle made me remember!' Excitedly she sang the words:

'Pesky weather, nothing goes right!
Pesky weather, lock the Doors tight!
Make a magic brew
With seven drops of dew,
A drop of thistle milk,
And a strand of spider silk.
Honey is the next thing—one full cup.
Use a stem of rosemary to mix it up.
Add a cup of rain,
Then mix again.
Add a sky-mirror flower,
Soak for half an hour.
Plant the stem straight and true,
Water with the brew,
Say, "Peskies all be gone!"
And your task is done.'

'Dew, thistle milk, spider silk – no problem,' muttered Patrice, writing busily. 'Honey . . . rosemary . . . a cup of rainwater – easy-peasey. It only rains at night, here, Jessie, but it *does* rain. And—?'

'A sky-mirror flower,' said Jessie triumphantly. She saw Patrice look puzzled, and her excitement faded. 'At least, I think that's what the words are,' she added. 'Maybe I heard them wrong.'

'You might have, dearie,' Patrice said slowly. 'I've never heard of a sky-mirror flower. Have you, Maybelle?'

Maybelle shook her head. 'If there is such a thing, it doesn't grow around here,' she said. 'I know every flower within walking distance.' She licked her lips thoughtfully. 'And most of them are delicious, I must say,' she added.

'I've heard of the sky-mirror,' said Giff unexpectedly. 'It's a sort of tree.'

As Jessie, Maybelle, and Patrice stared at him in amazement, he pushed out his bottom lip. 'I do know *some* things, you know,' he said resentfully. 'My mother taught me everything she knew.'

'That wouldn't be much,' Maybelle muttered under her breath. Patrice frowned at her and Maybelle raised her eyebrows innocently.

'So, tell us about sky-mirror trees, Giff,' Jessie said eagerly. 'What do they look like? When do they have their flowers?'

Giff looked uncomfortable. 'Um—I don't know,'

he said, and winced as Maybelle made a rude, huffing sound.

'Never mind,' soothed Patrice, shooting a warning glance at Maybelle. 'Just tell us where in the Realm they grow.'

Giff licked his lips. 'Um—I don't know that, either,' he said.

'What *do* you know about sky-mirror trees, Giff?' Maybelle drawled.

'Um—nothing,' said Giff.

'Told you so,' Maybelle hissed smugly to Patrice. Patrice closed her eyes as if she was praying for patience. Then she opened her eyes again.

'Come on,' she said. 'We're going to tidy ourselves up, then we're going to the palace library. If we can't find a book there to tell us where to find a sky-mirror tree, I'll eat my apron.'

CHAPTER FOUR

The Library

he palace library was a vast, round room inside one of the palace towers. Its curved walls were lined with shelves that stretched all the way from the smooth marble floor to the glass roof high above. Teams of fairies dressed in pale blue were flying rapidly up and down the shelves, taking out books or putting them back in place.

The fairy librarians looked hot and flustered, and Jessie could see why. The library was very busy. The rows of long glass tables in the centre of the floor were piled high with books and crowded with the tall, finely dressed Realm people called the Folk.

The Folk were using their wands to make the

pages of their books turn rapidly. As each book was finished, it was tossed into the air for the fairy librarians to catch and put away. And more books were being added to the tables every minute.

'My word, there'll be some tired wings tonight,' said Patrice, watching one team of tiny fairies struggling upward with a huge red book that wasn't much smaller than Giff.

'Is the library always this crowded?' Jessie whispered.

'Goodness, no!' Patrice whispered back. 'But before she left, Queen Helena asked everyone to keep looking for the Peskie spell, in case the Furry-bears couldn't—'

'We should tell them they can stop now,' squeaked Giff. 'We should tell them that Jessie—'

'Shhh!' scolded a librarian fairy, zooming past his nose. 'Silence in the library! This is your final warning.'

'Unfriendly lot, aren't they?' Maybelle muttered as the fairy darted away.

'They're usually very nice,' said Patrice, looking rather flustered. 'They're just a bit frazzled today, I suppose. Look, let's just do what we came to do. Come on!'

She found a small empty space at the end of one

of the tables, and they squeezed into it, apologising to the Folk on either side of them, who frowned at the disturbance. There was only just room for them all. Patrice and Jessie sat down, Maybelle stood behind them, and Giff sat on Patrice's knee.

Patrice took a slip of pale blue paper from a pile on the table, picked up a silver pencil, and wrote: 'Trees of the Realm.' Then she held the paper up. Almost instantly, a team of fairies swooped down, snatched the paper from her hand, and soared away.

'Now what?' whispered Giff, wriggling impatiently.

'We wait,' Patrice whispered back. 'Sit still!'

In a minute or two the fairies returned, almost hidden beneath a large, thick book. As they put the book down in front of Patrice, Jessie saw that the title was *Trees of the Realm A–Z*. It was very dusty and had a faded painting of a fairy-apple tree in full bloom on the cover. It looked as if no one had opened it for a very long time.

'You look, Jessie,' whispered Patrice, pushing the book over to Jessie. 'You'll be quicker than I will.'

'It's got no pictures inside,' said Giff in disappointment, as Jessie began leafing quickly through the book, looking for trees beginning with S.

'What does that matter?' Maybelle snapped. 'We don't need pictures, we need information.'

'Keep your voices down, for goodness' sake,' hissed Patrice. 'Do you want to get us thrown out?' She sneezed as dust from the book flew up and tickled her nose. 'Bless me,' she murmured and felt for her handkerchief.

Jessie found the S section. She started to turn the pages more slowly, running her finger down the paragraphs of small print to make sure she didn't miss what she was looking for.

'Sail Tree . . .' she read under her breath. 'Sausage Tree . . . Seven-Flower Tree . . . Shadow Gum . . . Silent Willow . . . Silver Elm . . .'

Patrice sneezed again. And again. Giff jiggled restlessly. Maybelle snorted, and nudged them both. They turned around to her, whispering crossly.

Trying to ignore them, Jessie turned a page and saw that lying between the next two pages was a piece of broad pink ribbon. Whoever had read this book last had obviously used the ribbon as a bookmark, then forgotten about it. But why was this particular page marked? Could it be . . .?

She felt a little thrill of excitement. Rapidly she ran her eye down the entries on the left-hand page, then pulled the pink ribbon aside so she could begin on the right.

Skallywag Ash . . . she read. *Skinny Oak . . .*

Skipping-Rope Tree . . . Then her heart thudded as she saw the next entry. *Sky-Mirror Tree.*

'It's here!' She gasped.

The whispered argument stopped abruptly. Patrice and Giff swung around and everyone bent to look at the place marked by Jessie's finger. Jessie read with rising excitement:

'Sky-Mirror Tree

The only sky-mirror tree in the Realm grows in the centre of Dally Glade. Its five-petalled, daisylike flowers appear throughout the year. They are very unusual because . . .'

Jessie looked up in surprise as Maybelle, Patrice, and Giff groaned. 'What is it?' she asked.

'We're doomed! Doomed!' wailed Giff. 'Oh, what are we going to do now?' His voice echoed loudly around the enormous room. The reading Folk all raised their heads from their books and frowned.

'Uh-oh,' Maybelle muttered, looking up.

Blue-clad fairies were swooping down on them, shushing them furiously. Jessie snatched her hand away just in time to save it from being flattened as the tree book slammed shut.

'You had your warning,' one of the fairies whispered sternly as the others seized the book and carried it away. 'Please leave at once!'

The four friends had no choice but to do as they were told. They trailed out of the library, not daring to look behind them, but very aware of hundreds of pairs of curious eyes burning into the backs of their necks.

'What's wrong with you all?' Jessie demanded furiously as the library doors closed firmly behind them. 'That was so *embarrassing*! Why did you yell like that? We found out what we wanted to know. The book said that the sky-mirror tree blooms all year, and that it grows in the centre of Dally Glade—'

Maybelle curled her lip. 'Exactly,' she said.

Jessie glanced at Patrice and Giff, who were both looking miserable. 'Oh!' she gasped. 'Don't—don't you know where Dally Glade is?'

'Oh, yes.' Patrice sighed. 'Everyone in the Realm knows about Dally Glade. But it's a problem, Jessie. For a start—'

'For a start it's just about as far away from here as it's possible to be,' Maybelle broke in loudly. 'It's in the west—days and days away, even if we had transport, which we don't. And even if the Peskies would leave us alone while we travelled, which they won't.'

'We're doomed!' Giff whimpered. 'By the time we

get to Dally Glade and back there'll be a million zillion Peskies. And all the magic will be gone!'

'Stop it!' snapped Maybelle. 'Things are bad enough without you wailing and complaining, you fool of an elf! If Dally Glade is where the sky-mirror tree grows, Dally Glade is where we'll have to go. We'll just have to find a way.'

'I won't be able to come with you,' Jessie said reluctantly. 'I promised I'd be home by sunset. But listen, there's something I *can* do to help. I brought Granny's cloak of invisibility with me. You can borrow it for the journey. The Peskies won't see you if you cover yourselves with the cloak, will they?'

'No, they won't,' Patrice said slowly. 'Queen Helena put on her cloak before she left for Brill, and she got away without any trouble. But we've still got to find a way to get to Dally Glade quickly, Jessie. Walking is out of the question. It would take much too long.'

'Wings!' Jessie exclaimed. 'You could borrow some wings and fly there!'

'I don't think wings will work under a cloak, dearie.' Patrice sighed.

'A good thing, too,' muttered Maybelle. 'I look ridiculous in wings.'

'Maybelle, how can you worry about what you

look like at a time like this?' Patrice exploded. 'Sometimes I really wonder—'

'Don't argue!' Jessie cried, holding up her hands pleadingly. 'We haven't got time. We have to think—'

Patrice gasped. Her black button eyes widened. 'Jessie, where did you get that?' she squeaked, pointing at Jessie with a trembling finger.

Bewildered, Jessie looked down and saw that she was still clutching the broad pink ribbon she had found in the library. 'This?' she said blankly, giving it to Patrice. 'Oh—it's nothing. I didn't realise I still had it. It was in the tree book, marking the page where the sky-mirror tree was.'

Patrice smoothed the ribbon between her work-worn fingers. Suddenly her face was shining. 'Oh, Maybelle! Giff! Look!' she whispered.

'I'm looking!' breathed Maybelle. 'And I can't believe my eyes!'

Giff's mouth was opening and closing, but no sound was coming out. He was gaping, fascinated, at the ribbon in Patrice's hand.

'What is it?' Jessie asked, very confused.

'It's a miracle!' Patrice sighed. 'Oh, Jessie, it's our answer! It's our way to Dally Glade. It's a Ribbon Road!'

CHAPTER FIVE

The Ribbon Road

I haven't seen a Ribbon Road for years!' Patrice chattered excitedly as she led the way back to her apartment. 'There were lots of them around at one time, but gradually they were all damaged or wore out. Queen Helena's went years ago—a griffin ate it, as I recall.'

'How does a Ribbon Road work?' Jessie panted, hurrying to keep up.

'You'll see,' said Maybelle. 'Now you can come with us, Jessie. We'll easily be back by sunset. In fact, we've got no choice. No one stays in Dally Glade once the sun goes down. It's forbidden.'

'What I'd like to know is how the Ribbon Road

got into that library book,' Patrice called over her shoulder before Jessie could ask what Maybelle meant. 'Imagine someone just forgetting where they'd left something so valuable!'

'It mightn't have been forgotten,' Jessie said. 'The ribbon was marking the page where the sky-mirror tree was. Maybe one of the Folk wanted to make sure that anyone who had to go to Dally Glade in an emergency would always have a way to get there.'

'I don't think so,' Maybelle snorted. 'The Folk aren't as careful as that. They never prepare for trouble—you can see that by the way they let the Peskie spell get forgotten. "All will be well," they say. And they believe it, too.'

Jessie laughed. Maybelle was right. 'All will be well' was one of her grandmother's favourite sayings. It was one of the things Jessie loved most about Granny, but it often made Rosemary shake her head in despair.

They reached Patrice's apartment and Jessie took the cloak of invisibility from her backpack while Patrice threw a bottle of water and some apples into a small cloth bag.

'Watch out for Peskies,' Maybelle warned. But whether it was because of the strong smell of orange juice, or because the Peskies were just hiding, there were no accidents.

'Now, we'll have to leave by my door because all the other doors in the palace are sealed against the Peskies,' Patrice said, quickly tying the little bag of provisions around her waist. 'And we won't be able to use the Ribbon Road at first. It won't work too close to the palace. We'll hide under Jessie's cloak till we get far enough away. Where do you think we should start the Road off, Maybelle?'

'The safest place would be beside the treasure house, where the griffins are,' Maybelle said, after thinking for a moment. 'The Peskies tend to keep away from there. The griffins ate quite a few of them yesterday.'

Giff moaned. And Jessie felt a knot in her stomach at the thought of facing the fierce griffins—even under a cloak of invisibility.

Giff and Jessie stood on either side of Maybelle, and Patrice stood at the little horse's head and spread the magic cloak over them all. Keeping together, they walked slowly into the hallway and checked in Patrice's long mirror to make sure that they were completely covered.

'I can still see your tail, Maybelle,' said Patrice, her voice muffled beneath the cloak. 'Can you curl it underneath you or something?'

'No, I can't,' said Maybelle crossly. 'The cloak just isn't big enough for all of us. Giff will have to stay here.'

'No,' Patrice said. 'Giff has to come. We need him.'

'*You're* the one who should stay home, Maybelle,' Giff said. 'Dally Glade's no place for a—'

'Don't you tell *me* what to do!' snapped Maybelle.

'It's all right,' Jessie said hurriedly. She tweaked the cloak and managed to arrange it so that even Maybelle's tail was completely invisible.

Cautiously Patrice opened the door and peeped out. The smell of orange juice was still very strong, and there were no Peskies to be seen.

As quietly as they could, the four friends slipped outside and began shuffling toward the back of the palace. They passed the path that led away into the Water Sprites' wood, reached the corner of the palace, and began to move around behind it.

The wind was wild. Bent almost double, Jessie struggled to hold the cloak in place. As it flapped around her, she could see Peskies jumping up and down on the roof of the food storehouse, bouncing on the branches of trees, and swarming all over the flowers.

Some tree branches had already cracked under their weight. Flowers were bruised and crushed. There were several large holes in the storehouse roof, and Jessie could hear bumps, crashes and high-pitched giggles coming from inside.

'Oh, no!' Maybelle groaned softly. 'I hope they haven't got into the oats.'

'Be quiet!' Patrice whispered. 'Do you want them to hear you?'

Painfully slowly, they shuffled on. And then at last Jessie heard the screeching roar of a griffin, and knew that they had nearly reached the treasure house. In one way, she was very relieved. In another way, she was scared to death. She shuddered at the thought of the griffins: four hideous winged beasts that were half lion, half eagle.

They're Queen Helena's pets, she told herself. But this didn't make her feel any better. Queen Helena was far away in Brill, and everyone knew that the griffins didn't obey anyone else.

'Get ready,' she heard Patrice mutter. 'We're nearly there. In a moment I'll unroll the Ribbon Road. Everyone has to put at least one foot on it. We'll have to come out from under the cloak to do that, so be sure to move fast. I'll count three, then everyone say, "Dally Glade." All right?'

'Yes,' Jessie murmured. She felt as if butterflies were flying around in her stomach. She was terrified that somehow she'd do something wrong and be left alone at the treasure house with masses of Peskies on one side and four angry griffins on the other.

'Right. Stop!' said Patrice. Jessie felt the cloak pull tight as the little housekeeper bent to unroll the pink ribbon on the ground. 'Now, everyone step on!' Patrice whispered. 'Quickly, now. One of the griffins is coming to see what we're up to.'

Jessie pulled off the invisibility cloak and looked around wildly. Patrice, Maybelle, and Giff were standing one behind the other, blinking in the light. They all had at least one foot planted on the pink ribbon. Behind them, the end of the ribbon flapped gaily in the breeze.

'Jessie!' wailed Giff. 'Hurry! Get on!'

Jessie tucked the invisibility cloak under her arm and tried to stand on the end of the ribbon. It flapped away from her foot. Desperately she tried again, and managed to stamp on it.

'All right!' she shrieked. The griffin's roars were deafening now. Jessie's hair was blowing around her face so that she could hardly see. But she could see enough to know that the griffin was lunging toward them, its cruel beak gaping wide, and its vast wings spread. She shut her eyes. She couldn't bear to look.

'One-two-three!' gabbled Patrice.

'Dally Glade!' Jessie shouted with everyone else.

And then, suddenly, they were flying—or, not flying, Jessie thought in confusion, but gliding, gliding very fast, as though they were skimming on ice. Wind was beating against her face. She could feel her legs moving, as though she were walking. Yet she wasn't bumping into Giff, who had been standing right in front of her. What was happening?

Fearfully, she opened her eyes. Patrice, Maybelle, and Giff were walking in front of her. They seemed to be walking at a normal speed, yet Giff's hair and Maybelle's mane and tail were streaming behind them, and the woods and meadows on either side of them were rushing past in a blur of green.

Jessie looked down. Beneath her feet was a broad, shining pink band. It was far wider than the little piece of ribbon she had found in the library. It was longer, too—much, much longer—and it was moving. It was stretching ahead into the distance, shining like a stream of fast-running water.

Jessie risked a quick glance over her shoulder. Behind her, the tail of the pink ribbon was curling up and disappearing as it was no longer needed.

She looked ahead again and caught a glimpse of the tip of the Ribbon Road winding up a hill like a snake. And then, in a blink, she herself was rushing up the hill and down the other side, while the Road streaked on toward the west.

'Try to think happy thoughts!' shouted Patrice over the wind. 'It'll help us go faster.'

Jessie did her best. But it was hard to feel lighthearted when there was so much to worry about. What was in store for them in Dally Glade? What if they couldn't find the sky-mirror tree? They didn't even know what it looked like!

And it was hard to relax on the Ribbon Road. She couldn't rid herself of the fear that she'd fall off. Never had she known such speed—not even on an amusement park ride. The feeling was terrifying and wonderful, both at once. Everything was a blur—a blur of speed and rushing sound.

So when at last she felt herself slowing down, and finally stopping, she felt startled and confused, as if she'd just woken from a dream. She blinked around her, only half seeing the shapes of trees and the figures of her friends.

'Everybody off!' she heard Patrice call. 'We're here!'

CHAPTER SIX

In Dally Glade

essie stumbled off the Ribbon Road. Her head was spinning. The ground under her feet seemed to be moving. She heard a high wail and a soft thump beside her.

'Get up, Giff!' she heard Maybelle say. Then she felt Patrice's hand on her arm. 'The giddiness will wear off in a minute, dearie,' Patrice murmured in her ear. 'Just take your time.'

Jessie took a couple of deep breaths. Slowly her head cleared and she could see what was happening around her. Giff was staggering to his feet, groaning and holding his head. Patrice was rolling up a small piece of pink ribbon. Maybelle was standing rigidly still, staring ahead. Jessie turned to see what she was looking at.

It was a huge grove of trees—trees of every shape and kind, rising from a rich green carpet of velvety moss. Some of the trees were tall and straight; some were graceful and spreading. Some had glossy, dark green leaves. Some had leaves so pale that the sun shone through them. Others were a mass of yellow, orange and red.

There was no wind. There were no Peskies, either. The only sound was a strange, soft whispering. The air was tingling with magic.

'What *is* this place?' Jessie whispered. The sun was warm, but she could feel herself shivering. She couldn't tear her eyes away from the mysterious forest. More than anything, she wanted to move into its shade, set her feet upon that soft, green moss, and walk among those whispering trees. And yet she was afraid.

She could see that her friends were uneasy, too. Patrice's hands were trembling as she tucked the pink ribbon away in her pocket. Giff was pale and silent. Even Maybelle was looking nervous.

'One of every kind of tree in the Realm grows in Dally Glade,' Patrice said in a low voice. 'It's a place of safety.'

'It doesn't feel very safe to me,' Jessie murmured.

'I mean it's safe for the trees,' Patrice said, glancing quickly at Maybelle. 'It's very well guarded. We'll have to be careful, and we'll have to be quick. It's getting late. Leave your pack here, Jessie. It's better not to be seen carrying anything. Then they won't think we mean any harm.'

'Who—?' Jessie began. But just then Patrice looked over her shoulder and gave a low cry.

Giff had moved silently away from them and was walking toward the forest.

'Giff, stop! Wait for us!' hissed Patrice, but Giff showed no sign that he had heard her. His eyes were open, but he looked like someone walking in a dream. His hands were tightly clasped. His face was awe-struck.

Jessie, Patrice and Maybelle ran after him and caught up with him just as he stepped into the whispering shade of the first trees. Patrice grabbed his arm, but Giff just kept walking, pulling her along with him. Maybelle gave an angry snort and plunged after them.

Jessie stuffed the cloak of invisibility into her backpack, and dropped the pack on the ground. Then she stepped forward, and the trees closed in around her.

It was like entering another world—a shady, green world that smelled of leaves and sap and growing things. Small pools of golden sunlight dappled the rich moss carpet. Branches made a roof over her head. Soft whispering filled the air.

Maybelle was just disappearing behind a tree with a slender black trunk and heart-shaped red leaves. The tree was like the ones that grew beside the palace treasure house. Her heart pounding, Jessie hurried to catch up. She had no wish to be alone in this strange place. She fell in line behind Maybelle. Ahead she could see Patrice, still holding Giff's arm as he threaded his way through the trees.

On they walked, and on, their feet making no sound on the soft moss carpet. The whispering grew louder, filling Jessie's ears and her mind. Soon she lost track of time. It was hard to remember why she was in the forest at all, and after a while she stopped trying. It was far easier just to walk, drinking in the beauty around her— the whispering trees, no two alike, the carpet of moss, vivid green, dotted with sunlight . . .

And then, in slow surprise, Jessie realised that the pools of golden light had disappeared. Frowning slightly, she looked up. Through the gaps in the leafy canopy above her she saw that the blue of the sky had faded. How did it get so late? she thought dreamily. How long have we been here?

Be indoors by sunset. . . . Her mother's words rushed into her mind like a splash of cold water. And then she remembered another voice— Maybelle's voice. *No one stays in Dally Glade once the sun goes down.*

Jessie felt a stab of fear. She looked ahead and saw the patch of white that was Maybelle moving along a narrow brown track that curved behind a tangle of black branches and red, heart-shaped leaves. Her stomach lurched.

'Maybelle!' she shouted. 'Wait!' She ran forward and touched Maybelle's shoulder. The little horse turned her head slowly. Her eyes were blank. Giff and Patrice had stopped and were looking around, too. Their eyes were as blank as Maybelle's.

'Wake up!' Jessie pleaded, shaking Maybelle violently. 'Giff! Patrice! Maybelle! Wake up!'

Maybelle licked her lips. 'We *are* awake,' she said thickly.

'You're not!' cried Jessie, shaking her again. 'Or not properly, anyway. We've all been walking in some sort of dream. Look!' She pointed to the tree with scarlet leaves and black branches. 'We've been beside this tree before! We saw it at the very beginning, and I think we've passed it a few more times since without realising it. See? We've made a little track in the moss. We've been walking in circles!'

Maybelle's brow creased. She looked at the brown earth beneath her feet and licked her lips again. Then, suddenly, she shivered and shook herself all over. At the same moment, Patrice and Giff gasped and began rubbing their eyes.

'They tricked us,' Patrice mumbled. 'Oh, I thought they'd give us a chance to explain, at least!'

'Who?' shouted Jessie, stamping her foot. '*Who* tricked us?'

'Shhh,' breathed a whispering voice right beside her. 'Sspeak ssoftly, human child.'

Jessie whirled around. At first she couldn't see where the voice had come from. Then her eye caught a movement, and she saw that a strange and beautiful being was sitting on a low branch of the red-leafed tree, right beside her.

The being had smooth black skin, and her slender body was clothed in scarlet silk. Her arms twined gracefully around the slim branches of the tree as if she were part of it. Heart-shaped red leaves were threaded in her long black hair.

Jessie stared in astonishment. Her first thought

was that the being had appeared out of thin air. Then she realised that this wasn't so. It was just that the being looked so like the tree she sat in that if she hadn't spoken and moved, she would have been perfectly disguised.

'Have you been here all along?' Jessie burst out. 'Are you the one who's been leading us in circles?'

'Yesss,' the being answered in a slow, whispering voice. 'I and my ssissters. But now the game is over. The ssun is ssetting, and we musst ssleep. Leave uss, and take the Danger with you.'

'W–what danger?' Jessie stammered, looking wildly around. 'We don't—'

'I think she means me,' said Maybelle flatly. 'She's a dryad, Jessie—a tree fairy. She thinks I'm a danger to trees.'

'You *are* a danger to trees,' Giff quavered. 'You eat leaves, don't you?'

Maybelle tossed her head. 'Occasionally,' she said. She was trying to sound offhand, but Jessie could tell that she was feeling very uncomfortable.

No wonder. The dryad was glaring, and the sound of whispering had suddenly grown very loud.

Jessie looked from side to side, and her eyes widened. Dryads were staring down at them from every tree. Every dryad looked different, because every one was like the tree in which she lived. One had curly brown hair, brown skin and a stiff, shiny green dress that exactly matched her tree's leaves. Another, who was in a spreading tree with soft golden leaves, had creamy white skin, wispy fair hair, and robes of the palest gold. A third, whose small tree was covered in bunches of bright orange berries, wore orange petticoats beneath her green skirt. She had a round, cheery-looking face, but she wasn't smiling now.

'Dryads, please listen!' Patrice begged. 'We mean the trees no harm. We have come here because the Realm is in terrible trouble.' She took Giff's arm and pulled him forward a little. 'As you can see, Giff the elf is one of us,' she went on. 'Surely you know that elves are tree-friends?'

The dryads nodded, but their serious expressions did not change. 'For all we know, you have brought the elf with you by force,' said the one in the red-leafed tree. 'Let him sspeak. We know he will not lie to usss.'

If Patrice felt insulted by these words, she didn't show it. She nodded encouragingly to Giff, who looked as if he might faint with fright.

'Sspeak, ssmall elf!' said the dryad with the curly brown hair.

Giff's ears were drooping almost to his shoulders. He was shaking all over. His mouth opened and closed, but no sound came out.

'Come on, Giff,' Jessie whispered desperately. 'You've got to do this! You're the only one who can help us now.'

CHAPTER SEVEN

Sky-Mirror

Giff made a huge effort to pull himself to-gether. 'Peskies!' he said in a strangled voice.

'Pesskiess!' The dryads leaned forward, their faces troubled.

'Millions of them,' Giff croaked. 'They're eating the magic, hurting the trees, hurting everything. Soon—soon they'll spread here as well. We—we found a spell to make them go away. But to make it we need—we need . . .'

His voice dried up. He gulped.

'We need a flower from the sky-mirror tree,' Jessie burst out, unable to keep silent any longer.

There was a shocked silence. Then the dryad with

the orange petticoats put her head on one side and stared at Jessie. 'Who are you, to sspeak of taking a flower from Dally Glade?' she asked bluntly. 'My tree and I sseem to know you, yet thiss cannot be.'

'This is Jessie, granddaughter of our true queen, Jessica,' Patrice said quickly. 'She looks very like Jessica did when she was young.'

'Ahh,' the dryads breathed. 'Jesssica . . .'

'Do you know my grandmother?' Jessie asked eagerly.

The dryad in the orange petticoats smiled. 'Princesss Jesssica came here many times,' she said. 'She came by a Ribbon Road, as you did. She was a true tree-friend. And sso was the human man she loved. At firsst we ssuspected he was a Danger, as many humans are. But he wanted only to make pictures of uss.'

Jessie nodded, suddenly certain she knew who had left the Ribbon Road in the tree book. It was just the sort of careful, sensible thing her grand-father would have done.

The dryads had begun whispering together. The whispering grew and spread, until it seemed that every tree in Dally Glade was rustling its leaves.

Jessie waited, in a fever of impatience. Blushes of rosy pink were now staining the sky. The sun was setting. She couldn't help thinking about what her mother was going to say to her when she got home.

If I get home, she thought suddenly, looking around at the serious faces of the dryads. What if they decide we're not telling the truth? They might keep us wandering around in this forest forever!

The whispering stopped, and the dryad in the red-leafed tree turned to Giff. 'We have decided to trusst you,' she said. 'Sso we will guide you to Ssky-Mirror. Pesskies are a threat to all of uss, but only Ssky-Mirror can decide to give one of her blooms for the sspell.'

'Come thiss way,' called the fair-haired dryad, beckoning gracefully. 'You musst hurry. No sstranger has ever been in our Glade sso late, sso near to darknesss. Take care the Danger does no harm.'

Very aware that they were being closely watched, Jessie, Giff, Patrice and Maybelle passed the golden tree, then moved on toward the centre of the forest. This time their path was made easy. The moss was springy, and seemed to hurry them along. Branches moved aside to let them pass, and a dryad leaned from every tree, pointing the way.

None of them had any idea what the sky-mirror tree looked like, and yet, the moment they saw it, they all knew it at once. It was smaller than the trees that surrounded it, though its gnarled trunk and spreading branches looked very old. Its soft green leaves were almost hidden beneath masses of beautiful pink daisy flowers. Magic seemed to stream from it, mingled with a delicious perfume that reminded Jessie of orange blossom.

Sitting on a low branch was a sweet-faced dryad with long brown hair. She was watching the strangers' approach intently.

'You and Giff go ahead, Jessie,' Patrice muttered, stopping abruptly. 'Maybelle and I will wait here.'

'Are you afraid I'll lose my head and grab a few sky-mirror leaves for dinner or something?' Maybelle snorted, baring her teeth. 'What do you think I am?'

'It's what the dryad thinks that matters,' Patrice hissed back. 'Stop scowling, Maybelle! Or at least stop showing your teeth!'

Jessie took Giff's hand and led him to the ancient tree. Beneath its canopy, the air had a faint pink glow, and was heavy with the sweet, magical perfume. The dryad sat absolutely still, almost invisible in her bower of pink and green.

Jessie's knees were trembling, and shivers were running up and down her spine. She glanced at Giff and saw that his eyes were filled with awe. She knew that he wouldn't be able to say a word. She took a deep breath.

'Greetings, Sky-Mirror,' she said in a low voice. 'We have come—'

'Shhh, Jesssie,' the dryad whispered. 'There is no need to sspeak. My ssissters have told uss who you are, and what you wishh.' Lovingly, she caressed the flowers above her head with long, slim fingers. Jessie waited, biting her lip.

'My tree and I have sspoken of your quesst,' whispered Sky-Mirror. 'Our flowers are precious to uss. Yet ssometimes we shhed one, as a gift of love to a sspecial friend. Our lasst gift was long ago. And it is longer sstill ssince we gave a bloom for the Pesskie sspell. But we remember. Ah, yess. We remember.'

The leaves of the tree rustled as if stirred by a soft breeze. The dryad stretched out her cupped hand and onto the palm fell one perfect pink bloom. Smiling, she leaned forward and gave the flower to Jessie.

Weak with relief, Jessie stammered her thanks. Then, holding the flower carefully, she backed away from the tree. Tugging Giff's hand to make him follow, she turned and ran back to where Patrice and Maybelle were waiting.

'You did it, Jessie!' said Patrice as she took the flower from Jessie's hand and put it in a silk-lined box she had brought especially for the purpose.

'I did it, too,' said Giff, finding his voice at last.

'Of course you did,' said Patrice, quelling Maybelle's disdainful snort with a sharp look. 'We couldn't have done it without you.'

They followed their own tracks back through the forest, surrounded by the whispered farewells of the dryads who leaned from their trees to watch them pass. At the forest's edge, Patrice unrolled the Ribbon Road once more.

'The return trip won't take long,' she said as everyone stepped on to the shining pink band. 'There'll be no shortage of happy thoughts this time.'

'Yes!' whooped Giff. 'Now you can make the brew, Patrice, and by morning the Peskies will be gone!'

'We still need a stem of rosemary,' Maybelle pointed out, clearly tired of being left out of things. 'There's a big old rosemary bush near the treasure house, I remember. We can get a stem from there.'

'Oh, that old bush died ages ago, Maybelle,' said Patrice. 'But Queen Helena's planted a new bush, right outside the palace kitchens. We'll get what we need from there.'

'Hmff!' snorted Maybelle, and Jessie felt a twinge of sympathy. First the dryads of Dally Glade had regarded the little horse as a menace, and now even her suggestion about the rosemary had proved to be mistaken.

But Giff, Patrice, and Jessie herself were far too happy for Maybelle's injured pride to slow down the Ribbon Road. As Patrice had promised, the return trip seemed to take no time at all. The glorious sunset was only just fading as they reached the treasure house and ran beneath Jessie's cloak to Patrice's apartment.

When they got there, they were surprised to find Queen Helena sitting at the kitchen table with her head in her hands.

'I used the key under the mat, Patrice,' Queen Helena said, after she'd recovered from her own shock at seeing Patrice, Maybelle, Giff, and Jessie suddenly appear from beneath the cloak. 'I just had to rest quietly for a while before I faced the Folk in the palace. I hope you don't mind.'

'Of course not,' exclaimed Patrice. 'It's wonderful you're back, your majesty. We—'

'Oh, Patrice, the Furrybears were no help at all!' Queen Helena broke in despairingly. 'They were so excited they just kept telling me story after story about all sorts of things. I must have heard thousands before I finally got away. But none of them were about the Peskie spell.'

She sighed. 'By the way, there are some Peskies in here, did you know? I found out when I tried to make some hot chocolate. I'll have some more milk sent to you from the palace kitchen. I'm sorry about the milk jug.'

'Queen Helena, it doesn't matter!' Patrice laughed. 'Nothing matters! Everything's going to be all right. We've got the spell, thanks to Jessie.'

Queen Helena blinked in shock, and her beautiful green eyes seemed suddenly to focus on Jessie's smiling face. 'Jessie!' she exclaimed. 'How did you get here? The Doors are locked! And what's all this about the spell?'

'It's a long story.' Jessie grinned. 'Patrice, Giff and Maybelle will tell you all about it. But in the meantime, Queen Helena, could you please magic me home? Right now?'

'Of course,' said Queen Helena, clearly very confused, but beginning to smile. 'Are you ready?'

Jessie grabbed the cloak of invisibility from the floor and stuffed it into her pack. 'Ready!' she said.

'We'll let you know what happens, dearie,' called Patrice. 'We'll send a flower fairy—'

Helena raised her hand. And before Jessie had time to do more than call goodbye to Giff, Patrice and Maybelle, darkness had closed in around her.

When she opened her eyes, she was standing in the secret garden. The first star was glimmering in the grey sky. Late, but not too late, Jessie thought in relief. Thank goodness!

She heard her mother calling her. She shouted an answer and ran for the house. Her mind was so full of exciting memories of her amazing day that she hardly noticed that her legs were stiff and aching. And she didn't hear the tiny chirruping sounds coming from her backpack at all.

CHAPTER EIGHT

The Demonstration

hat night, Jessie lay awake for a long time, hoping for news from the Realm. But no fairy messenger appeared at her window, and finally she fell asleep, to have vivid, troubling dreams of wandering in a forest where the trees had come to life.

She woke exhausted and aching in every muscle. She just couldn't make herself get out of bed. When finally she did, she had no time to do more than throw on the clothes she'd put out the night before, gobble some breakfast, grab her backpack and run.

She arrived at school very out of breath, and made it to her classroom just as Ms Stone was calling the roll. Gratefully she sank into her usual place beside Sal, who grinned broadly, raised her eyebrows, and nodded silently toward the front of the classroom.

Jessie looked, and her jaw dropped. A ladder was leaning against the wall beside the blackboard, which was still covered with the list of superstitions the class had made the previous Friday.

'This morning we're going to finish talking about superstitions,' Ms Stone said crisply, walking to the door. 'Please take out your pens and workbooks, and turn to the notes you made on Friday.'

Ignoring the excited whispering that began the moment she turned her back, she opened the door, looked out, and beckoned.

'I bet she's going to make us all walk under that ladder,' Sal hissed as Jessie bent to get her pen out of her pack.

'Oh, no! She wouldn't!' whispered Lisa Wells in horror.

Jessie was hardly listening. She'd just realised that the cloak of invisibility was still in her pack. She'd forgotten all about it. Hoping that no one would notice, she dug deep beneath the folds of soft fabric, feeling around for her pen case.

Ms Stone ushered in a very small boy holding a very large cat carrier. 'This is Michael Tan from

Year Two,' she announced. 'As you may know, Year Two is having its pet show today. Michael has been very kind and agreed to let his pet help us with our demonstration before the pet show begins.'

Michael Tan nodded briskly and pushed his large spectacles back on his nose. He didn't seem at all over-awed to be the centre of attention. He put the cat carrier on the floor, opened it, and lifted out a fat, sleepy-looking black cat with a stubby tail. The cat didn't so much as twitch its whiskers, but lay draped across Michael's arms, absolutely limp, like a furry cushion with legs.

'Tell us your cat's name, Michael,' said Ms Stone, frowning as the class began to whisper again, and everyone at the back half stood, craning their necks to see.

'Hith name ith Mithster Black,' the boy said, in a high, piercing voice. 'He likes thleeping and food. He'th only got half a tail, becauthe a long time ago Dad mowed the end of it off by mithtake. He'th theventeen yearth old, and Mum thays he'll prob'ly die thoon.'

'Right,' said Ms Stone hurriedly as some of the class tittered. 'Thank you, Michael.'

Jessie's fingers closed around her pen case. As she began to pull it out, she heard something that made

166

the blood rush to her face. It was a soft, chirruping sound. It was horribly familiar. And it was coming from inside her backpack.

Jessie froze, her mind flying back to her last minutes in Patrice's kitchen, to the cloak lying unguarded on the floor. She remembered how she'd pushed the cloak into her pack in a hurry. She hadn't checked it for Peskies. She hadn't dreamed . . .

'Jessie, what are you doing down there?' Sal whispered. 'You're missing everything!'

Jessie jerked out her pen case and bumped the back of her head on the edge of the table. Seeing stars, she fumbled with the zipper on her pack, frantically trying to close it.

The zip stuck halfway. As Jessie struggled with it, two small green creatures with wings hopped gleefully out of the pack, bounced twice on the back of her hand, then leaped off and disappeared beneath the table. With a gasp, Jessie dived after them. But the Peskies had hidden. She couldn't see them anywhere.

'Jessica!' snapped Ms Stone from the front of the room.

Pink-faced and breathing hard, Jessie scrambled from under the table. 'Sorry, Ms Stone,' she mumbled. 'I—I dropped something.'

'Well, just leave it for now,' said Ms Stone sharply. 'It won't run away. Are you ready, Michael?'

The boy nodded, and plumped the cat on the ground. It crouched where it landed, looking even more like a furry cushion than it had before.

'Now,' said Ms Stone. 'On our board we have a list of things that are supposed to cause bad luck. I am going to prove to you, once and for all, that they do not. Sally! Stand up, please.'

The smirk disappeared from Sal's face. She jumped to her feet, and her chair toppled backward and hit the floor with a crash. Lisa Wells screamed.

'That was not bad luck, Lisa,' said Ms Stone icily. 'It was sheer clumsiness.'

It was Peskies, Jessie thought. As she helped Sal pick up the chair, she tried to peer under the table without Ms Stone noticing. She thought she caught a glimpse of green out of the corner of her eye, but when she looked again, it had gone.

'Sally, please read out the items on the board,' Ms Stone said, taking a small green umbrella from her table. 'Stop after each one. I'll tell you when to go on.'

Her eyes wide, struggling to keep her mouth from twitching into a grin again, Sal read. 'It is bad luck to walk on the cracks in the pavement.'

'We have no cracks in the classroom floor,' Ms Stone said, with a small smile. 'But I stepped on every crack in the path on my way up from the car park this morning. I called Isaac to walk with me, and he was my witness. Weren't you, Isaac?'

Everyone turned to look at Zac Janowsky. He went red. 'Yes,' he said loudly. His friends all grinned and nudged one another.

'Go on, Sally,' said Ms Stone.

'It is bad luck to break a mirror,' said Sal. Ms Stone held up a small, cracked mirror, and told them she'd broken it before she left home.

'It is bad luck to walk under a ladder,' read Sal. Her voice quavered slightly as Ms Stone walked through the gap between the ladder and the wall. Ms Stone looked at her and nodded sharply.

'It is bad luck to spill salt, unless you throw a pinch of it over your shoulder afterward,' Sal said. Ms Stone took a container of salt from her pocket.

One of the overhead lights began to ping and flicker. Lisa squeaked and clapped her hand over her mouth. Everyone else started talking and giggling.

'Be quiet!' snapped Ms Stone, frowning. 'Now, this is exactly the sort of silliness I've been talking about! The light was due to fail, so it failed. That's all there is to it.'

Crossly, she twisted the top of the salt container to open it. The container slipped from her hand. It bounced on the floor, the lid flew off, and salt spilled everywhere.

At the same moment, one of the window blinds flew up with a clatter, and a poster fell off the wall.

Over the delighted shouts of the class, Jessie clearly heard the gleeful chirruping of Peskies making mischief. I have to make Ms Stone stop the demonstration, she thought wildly. I have to tell her we should leave the classroom.

But one glance at Ms Stone's face, now blotched with angry red patches, made her realise that she'd be silly even to try.

'Sally, go on,' said Ms Stone through tight lips.

'It is bad luck to open an umbrella in the house,' Sal read. She bit her lip to stop herself from laughing as Ms Stone opened the umbrella and held it over her head.

'And the next,' said Ms Stone grimly,

'It is bad luck if a black cat crosses your path,' said Sal, darting a look at Michael Tan and Mister Black.

'Go ahead, Michael,' said Ms Stone. Michael walked to the wall, so that he and his cat were on opposite sides of the door. Then he turned around and took the lid from a small plastic container. The strong, fishy smell of cat food filled the room. Michael put the open container on the floor in front of him.

'Mithter Black!' he called in his piercing voice. 'Fishies!'

The huge cat stirred. Its nose twitched. It heaved itself up and began to pad rapidly toward Michael.

Holding the green umbrella high, Ms Stone began to walk slowly toward the door. Intent on getting to his snack, Mister Black took no notice of her. He walked right in front of her, and buried his nose in the container.

Quite a few people cheered, and Michael Tan beamed as if his cat had done some amazing trick.

'Settle down, please,' said Ms Stone from the door. She was closing the green umbrella. The red patches on her cheeks and forehead were slowly fading. 'Sally, you can sit down now. And, Michael, you can go back to class. Thank you very much for your help.'

Without ceremony, Michael jerked the plastic box away from Mister Black and stood up. Mister Black made a huffing sound and slowly turned his head from one side to the other, as if wondering where the food had gone.

'That is the stupidest cat!' Sal whispered to Jessie, sinking into her chair. Jessie didn't answer. Cold with horror, she was looking at the Peskie dancing on Michael Tan's right shoe.

CHAPTER NINE

Bad Luck

or homework tonight, I want everyone to write a one-page report on the demonstration you've just seen,' Ms Stone said. 'And I hope—'

She broke off as Zac Janowsky stuck his hand in the air and urgently pumped it up and down. 'Yes?' she asked impatiently.

'Something's crawling on his foot,' said Zac, pointing at Michael Tan.

And at that moment, Mister Black saw the Peskie, too. His fur stood on end. He sprang forward with a yowl, thudding down on Michael's feet with all four paws. Michael rocked backward, lost his balance and sat down abruptly. The container of cat food shot out of his hand and turned upside down, spilling its smelly contents on the floor.

Some people laughed. Some screamed. Jessie saw a green blur zoom toward the back of the room. Mister Black tore after it. It was hard to believe he was the same cat. His eyes were blazing. His fur was so fluffed up that he looked twice his normal size. He made a flying leap onto a table, scattering books and pens everywhere. The kids sitting around the table yelled and jumped up, their chairs crashing behind them.

Mister Black sprang onto the long, low cupboard that stood against the back wall. He raced along it, teeth bared. Clay models, paper masks and books went flying. A vase of flowers toppled and smashed, spraying water everywhere.

Dripping wet, and with a yellow chrysanthemum stuck behind his ear, Mister Black yowled and raced on, heading for the front of the room again.

'Catch him!' shouted Ms Stone, losing her composure at last. She dashed forward and trod in the mound of cat food. Her foot shot out from under her, and she grabbed the blackboard for support. As it crashed to the ground, bringing the screaming Ms Stone down with it, the classroom door flew open.

Mr Morris, the teacher from the class next door,

was standing there, his eyes bulging in amazement. Two tiny streaks of green darted past his ear, circled him three times, then sped out into the corridor, clicking excitedly. Mr. Morris's shirt came untucked, a button fell from his cardigan, and one of the lenses dropped out of his glasses. He blinked in astonishment.

Mister Black ran through the smeared cat food and skidded to a halt. His nose twitched. He sat down and began calmly licking his paws.

Sal and some of the others rushed out to help Ms Stone, but Jessie didn't move. She sat with her hands clasped tightly together, filled with guilt. Ms Stone was absolutely right about superstitions. It was Jessie's fault that the Peskies had escaped and caused havoc.

And now they're loose in the school, Jessie thought, panic stricken. Who knows what trouble they'll cause? I'll have to get back to the Realm as quickly as I can and get some of the magic brew. I'll have to think of an excuse to go home.

But she didn't need an excuse. Ms Stone was taken off to the hospital with a sprained ankle. Her classroom was a disaster area. In the end, the principal called all the class parents, suggesting that, if possible, their children should leave for the day.

'Poor Ms Stone. What a disaster!' Rosemary said when Jessie arrived home. 'I suppose Lisa and Rachel are saying it was all because she walked under a ladder and so on.'

'They are,' said Jessie gloomily. 'It's awful!'

'If she'd had an accident in six months' time, they'd have said the same thing,' Rosemary said absentmindedly, putting down the cookbook she'd been reading when Jessie came in. 'Look, Jessie, I'm just going to run up to the store for a minute. There's a recipe here for little apple cakes that I'd like to try, but it calls for green apples, and I've only got red ones here.'

'Wouldn't red ones do?' Jessie asked.

Her mother shrugged. 'Maybe,' she said. 'But maybe not. You've got to be careful with recipes you've never tried before. Anyway, it's a beautiful day—not a cloud in the sky. I'll be glad to get outdoors for a while. You should make the most of your free day, too, Jess.'

I will, Jessie thought, her mind already on the Realm. As her mother left the house, she hurried to her room. Her heart pounded when she saw a folded piece of blue paper lying on her desk.

Eagerly she snatched up the paper and unfolded it, but as she read the scrawled words, her heart sank.

Jessie—

The spell didn't work. We don't know why. We followed the recipe exactly. More Peskies here every minute. Don't come in again. Too dangerous. Don't worry about us.

P, M, & G

Jessie slumped down at her desk, shaking her head in bewildered dismay. Why hadn't the Peskie spell worked?

Obviously one of the ingredients was wrong, she thought. But which one? I'm sure I remembered the rhyme properly. I'm positive!

She propped her chin on her hands, and gazed through the window. Her mother was right. It was a glorious day. The rough wind had gone and the sky was a pure, clear blue—as blue as the sky of the Realm. But Jessie didn't feel like going outside. She didn't feel like doing anything at all.

There was a sound from the door. She turned to see Flynn stalking in, his tail held high. He sat down at her feet and looked at her inquiringly.

'I've messed things up, Flynn,' Jessie said miserably. 'But I don't know how!'

The sketchbook she'd taken from her grand-father's studio was still lying on the desk in front

177

of her. Idly she began looking through it, only half seeing the drawings and the leaves and flowers pressed between the pages. Granny's little song was running round and round in her mind.

> . . . *Add a cup of rain,*
> *Then mix again.*
> *Add a sky-mirror flower,*
> *Soak for half an hour . . .*

And at that very moment, she turned a page and caught a faint whiff of a delicious, strangely familiar scent. Jessie blinked, focused, and saw the small blue flower she'd looked at with Mrs Tweedie. She stared at it, frowning in puzzlement.

How strange! The whiff of perfume she'd caught as the page turned had reminded her of the orange-blossom scent of the sky-mirror tree.

'I'm imagining things now, Flynn,' Jessie said. She stared down at the flower in the book. It was the same shape as a sky-mirror bloom—a five-petalled daisy with a golden centre—but there the resemblance ended. The petals of the pressed flower were as blue as the sky outside Jessie's window, while the flowers of the sky-mirror tree had been pink. Jessie knew she'd never forget her first sight of that graceful mass of flowers that seemed to reflect the colour of the sunset sky above—

Sky-mirror!

Jessie gasped and sat bolt upright, gripping the edge of the desk. Suddenly she was remembering the words she'd read about the sky-mirror in *Trees of the Realm A–Z*.

Its five-petalled, daisy-like flowers appear throughout the year. They are very unusual because . . .

She'd been interrupted before she could read on. She'd never found out why sky-mirror flowers were so unusual. Now she thought she knew.

'This *is* a sky-mirror flower,' she whispered. 'Sky-Mirror gave it to my grandfather. It was one of her "gifts of love." And it's blue because—because the sky-mirror does what its name says. Its flowers reflect the sky. When the sky is blue, the flowers are blue. When the sky changes colour, the flowers change, too—to pink, or orange, or grey, or black . . .'

And what had her mother said in the kitchen just now: *You've got to be careful with recipes you've never tried before.*

Gently Jessie picked up the pressed flower. Her heart was beating very fast. Calm down, she told herself. This may not mean anything. The Peskie spell didn't say what colour the sky-mirror bloom had to be when it was used in the brew.

But then the words of the fair-haired dryad were ringing in her ears. *No sstranger has ever been in our Glade sso late, sso near to darknesss . . .*

'The rhyme didn't have to say the colour, Flynn,' she exclaimed. 'Dally Glade is forbidden to strangers once sunset begins. And any sky-mirror flower given during the day would have to be blue! The old Realm Folk who made up the rhyme took that for granted.'

The flower in the book was dry, and very old. Would it still work? There was no way of knowing, but Jessie knew she had to try.

She pulled open her desk drawer, found a little box that had once held paper clips, and put the pressed flower gently inside. Then she tucked the box carefully into her pocket, grabbed her cloak of invisibility from her pack, and ran to her grandmother's room.

Flynn padded after her. He watched gravely as she went to the magic painting. As she put on the cloak, he made a low, growling sound. Jessie glanced at him and bit her lip. 'It'll be all right, Flynn,' she whispered.

But she wasn't so sure. Her hands were trembling

as she pulled the cloak more closely around her. She faced the painting, and thought hard of Patrice's kitchen. 'Open!' she said.

The painting seemed to grow larger. And Jessie felt herself being swept toward it, swept into soft, chill darkness.

CHAPTER TEN

Surprises

essie screwed her eyes shut and tried to keep her mind focused on Patrice's kitchen. That's where I have to go, she thought. Patrice's kitchen. Nowhere else . . .

And then she suddenly realised that she had stopped moving. She was warm again. She could hear voices. And she could smell orange juice!

She opened her eyes cautiously, and with a stab of joy realised that she was where she had wanted to be. Patrice, wearing a red-chequered apron, was grimly squeezing oranges at the kitchen bench. Giff was hunched miserably at the table. Maybelle was pacing around, looking worried and irritable.

None of them glanced in Jessie's direction. She remembered that they couldn't see her, and threw off the cloak.

Giff screamed in shock. Patrice whirled around with a startled cry, sweeping a dozen oranges off the bench. The oranges began rolling all over the floor.

'Jessie!' roared Maybelle, stamping her foot. 'What are you *doing* here? Didn't we tell you—?'

'I had to come,' Jessie broke in. 'Listen!' And, as quickly as she could, she explained everything.

'I don't know if a dried sky-mirror flower works as well as a fresh one,' she finished, pushing the little box into Patrice's hands. 'But it's worth a try, isn't it?'

'It certainly is,' said Patrice, her black button eyes gleaming with new hope. 'Anything's worth a try now.'

She whirled round to the bench and swept the remaining oranges aside with a single movement of her plump arm. 'I've got all the other brew ingredients here,' she said, pointing to the row of jars and bottles at the back of the bench. 'All right. Let's start.'

With Jessie, Giff, and Maybelle clustered around her, she began measuring the brew ingredients into a blue-and-white-striped jug. Seven drops of dew, a drop of thistle milk, a piece of spider's web, a cup of honey . . .

'Pass me a piece of that rosemary, Jessie,' she said tensely.

Jessie passed over a fragrant stem of rosemary and watched as Patrice stirred the thick, golden mixture.

'Add a cup of rain, then mix again,' Maybelle prompted, pressing forward.

'I know, I know,' Patrice said impatiently, pulling the cork from a bottle labelled 'Rainwater' and carefully measuring out a cup of crystal clear liquid. She added the water to the brew and carefully stirred again. Slowly the mixture grew thinner, as the water and honey mixed together.

At last Patrice put the sticky stem carefully to one side. 'Now,' she said. She opened Jessie's little box and took out the sky-mirror flower. It looked very faded and fragile in her brown hand. Jessie crossed her fingers for luck, thought of Ms Stone, and gave a snort of nervous laughter.

Patrice dropped the flower into the golden brew. It lay on the surface, pale, dry, and lifeless.

'It's not going to work,' Giff groaned. 'Look at it! It's dead! Oh, doom!'

'Mix it in, Patrice,' urged Maybelle, nudging

Patrice's shoulder. 'It won't do any good just lying there.'

'No,' Patrice said firmly. 'I'm not going to touch it. The rhyme doesn't say to mix the flower in. It says to let it soak for half an hour, so that's what we'll do.' Ignoring Maybelle's snort of disgust, she turned a half-sized hourglass over. Fine silver sand began running from the top of the hourglass to the bottom.

'All right,' she went on, lifting her chin. 'Now I'm going to clean up this kitchen. You can all help me or not help me, as you like. But no one's to think about the brew again, or talk about it, or touch it, until the half hour's up.'

The little housekeeper's voice was strong, but Jessie could see that her eyes had lost their hopeful glint, and her own heart sank.

The next thirty minutes were the slowest Jessie had ever known. She helped Patrice wash up and put things away. Maybelle paced, lashing her tail. Giff crawled around the floor, picking up oranges, dropping them again, and getting under everyone's feet. They all kept looking at the hourglass. No one spoke.

At last, it was time. 'All right,' said Patrice. 'Let's look.'

The friends crept together to the kitchen bench. At the last moment, Jessie shut her eyes. She couldn't bear to look. Then she heard Giff squeal, Patrice gasp, and Maybelle give a high whinny of joy. She opened her eyes, and her heart leaped.

The sky-mirror flower had completely dissolved. And the mixture in the jug was no longer honey gold, but blue as the sky.

'The first brew didn't change colour, did it Patrice?' squealed Giff, jumping up and down. 'It didn't, did it? Did it?'

'No,' said Patrice, smiling broadly as she poured the blue mixture into a glass bottle and corked the bottle tightly. 'This time we've got the brew right—I'm sure of it. Oh, I think everything's going to be all right.'

❦

And everything *was* all right, though none of them was prepared for what happened when Queen Helena planted the rosemary stem in the rich earth beside the treasure house. Well-wrapped in her cloak of invisibility, with Jessie, Giff, Patrice, and Maybelle huddled close beside her beneath their own cloak, Helena pressed the stem firmly into place. Then she watered it with the blue liquid from Patrice's little glass bottle, and called in a ringing voice, 'Peskies all be gone!'

Alerted by the sound of her voice, Peskies began flying toward her from every direction. The four griffins lumbered forward, growling ferociously, snapping their beaks and spreading their enormous wings. 'Oh, paddywinks and sosslebones!' Jessie heard Patrice mutter.

'Patrice! Get back to the palace,' said Queen Helena urgently. 'All of you—go quickly! I'll hold them off for as long as I can.'

'No! We can't leave you here alone, your majesty!' Giff wailed, twisting to look at the approaching swarm. 'We'll defend you. We'll—'

'Look!' Jessie gasped. 'Look at the rosemary!'

Her eyes were wide with astonishment and wonder. The rosemary stem was growing! One minute it was standing small, straight and lonely in the brown earth. The next minute it was sprouting side branches and increasing in size so fast that in two blinks it had become a sturdy shrub as tall as Giff, and four times as wide.

Blue flowers burst into bloom among the new bush's spiky, dull green leaves. A tingling perfume—

similar to the scent that drifted in the secret garden, but many times stronger, and tinged with the scent of orange blossom—filled the air.

The Peskies stopped in midflight. They hovered uncertainly, wrinkling their tiny noses. Then, suddenly, they shrieked. Thousands of them shriveled up and blew away in the breeze like tiny shreds of dead grass. The rest turned and fled back to the hills, desperate to escape.

And as the breeze caught the magical scent and gently wafted it north, south, east, and west, dark clouds of Peskies rose into the sky from everywhere, and vanished like smoke.

'The old rosemary bush that was here had a scent like this,' Jessie heard Queen Helena murmur. 'Why, it must have been what was keeping the Peskies away for all these years. I was sad when it died, but I had no idea it was so special.'

'We did it!' Giff shrieked. 'We're saved!' He tore off the cloak of invisibility, and began capering wildly around the magic rosemary bush. The largest of the griffins roared angrily and bounded forward.

Queen Helena pulled off her own cloak. Seeing his beloved mistress suddenly appear before him, the griffin stopped, crouched, and wagged its lion's tail. Queen Helena scratched its curved beak affectionately. 'Go back to the treasure house now, Boris,' she said softly. 'There's a good boy.'

The griffin turned obediently and lumbered back to its post.

Folk had begun streaming from the palace, waving, cheering and celebrating. Sounds of joy were rising from the surrounding forests and fields as the people of the Realm gradually realised that the Peskie plague had ended.

'Jessie, you've been wonderful!' Queen Helena said. 'How can we ever thank you?'

'Do you think I could have a little bunch of the special rosemary?' Jessie asked eagerly. 'I'd like to take it to school tomorrow. We've got a bit of a Peskie problem there.'

Queen Helena laughed. 'Of course!' she said. 'And also, we mustn't forget . . .' She lifted her hand, and Jessie's charm bracelet made a tiny, jingling sound. Jessie looked down and saw that a new charm now hung from the gold chain. It was a five-petalled daisy. She beamed.

'Thank you,' she said. 'I'm so glad I could help.'

'Jessie always helps,' cried Giff, throwing his arms around Jessie's waist.

'Yes,' Patrice said fondly. 'I don't know how she does it!'

'I suppose she'd say it was all just a matter of human common sense,' Maybelle teased.

'Not this time,' Jessie smiled, looking down at her bracelet. 'This time it was magic. Pure magic. And a little bit of luck.'

A charm bracelet opens
a magical world of adventure

The Rainbow Wand

EMILY RODDA

CHAPTER ONE

Sticky-beak

he flower fairies whirled around Jessie in a fluttering blur of pink, blue, green, purple, yellow, and white. Their bright wings brushed Jessie's cheeks. Their tiny fingers tangled in her golden-red hair. Their voices rang in her ears like crystal bells.

'Don't go, Jessie! Queen Helena is in the west, and we've got no-one to dance with us. Stay in the Realm and dance with us, Jessie! Oh, please, please, please!'

'Rose! Bluebell! Violet! Daffodil! Daisy! Stop this!' Jessie laughed. 'I have to go back to my own world now. It's Saturday, and Mum's home. She'll be wondering where I am. I'll dance with you next time I visit, I promise.'

'But that won't be for a long time!' cried Daisy. 'That's what you said to Patrice the palace housekeeper, and Giff the elf, and Maybelle the little white horse.'

'You said you had to stay away from the Realm—because of a nasty old sticky-beak!' added Bluebell.

'Oh, you naughty fairies!' Jessie exclaimed. 'You were hiding! You were listening!'

Bluebell and Violet hung their heads, but Daffodil, Daisy, and Rose giggled.

'Yes,' said Daffodil, smoothing her yellow skirts. 'We were hiding in the Ding Dong tree and we heard. What's a sticky-beak, Jessie? What, what, what?'

'Someone who pokes her nose into other people's business!' said Jessie, trying hard to sound stern. She faced the shadowy archway that marked the border of the Realm. 'Open!' she called.

She closed her eyes as shadows surrounded her. Her skin prickled as the familiar cool, tingling breeze swept her away.

Then, suddenly, everything grew still again. She could hear birds singing. The tangy scent of rosemary filled the air.

Jessie opened her eyes. She was standing on a small square of smooth green grass. The grass was edged with rosemary bushes and surrounded by a high, clipped hedge. She was back in the place she called the secret garden. She was home.

Quickly she checked to see that the door in the hedge was still shut, and that the spade she'd wedged against the old latch was still firmly in place. She breathed a sigh of relief when she saw that everything was just as she'd left it.

No-one had tried to enter the secret garden while she was away. Now all she had to do was get back to the house without—

'Surprise!' squealed five tiny voices. And there were the flower fairies, dancing in the air in front of her, their faces filled with glee.

'We tricked you, Jessie!' shrieked Daffodil. 'We came with you!'

'Now you can dance with us *here*!' squeaked Rose, dipping and twirling so that her frilly pink skirts billowed out around her and the tails of her green sash flew.

'No, I can't!' said Jessie, hiding a smile. 'I have to go up to the house. Mum will be—'

Suddenly anxious, Jessie ran to the door in the hedge, opened it cautiously, and peered out. The

Blue Moon garden was deserted, except for the birds chattering in the trees. Her mother, Rosemary, was nowhere to be seen, and for once there was no sign of Louise Tweedie, their nosy next-door neighbour, either.

Jessie breathed a sigh of relief. It had been a good idea to visit the Realm today—the day when the inside of Mrs Tweedie's house was going to be painted. She'd hoped that Mrs Tweedie would be too busy fussing around the painters to be bothered about Blue Moon, and it looked as if she'd been right. Still . . .

She turned back to the fairies. 'You should go back to the Realm now,' she said. 'Someone might see you.'

Shy little Violet looked worried, but Daisy grinned. 'No-one sees us,' she boasted, swinging on a stem of rosemary. 'If they do, they think we're flutterbyes.'

'Flutterbyes, flutterbyes!' giggled Daffodil, opening and closing her yellow wings.

'They might think you're butterflies at first,' Jessie argued. 'But what if they look more closely? What if . . .?'

'Your grandmother, our true Queen, likes it when we come to her garden to play, Jessie,' Bluebell said seriously. 'And lately she has been making a new game—'

'I see one!' shrieked Rose. She darted under a rosemary bush, then fluttered back out onto the grass clutching something that looked like a tiny green-and-white-striped pillow.

'Sweetie-pies!'

With squeals of excitement, the other fairies began flying around, searching for more hidden treats.

'Quickly, quickly!' squeaked Daffodil. 'Find them all before the rainbow fairies come and find them first! Emerald said that they found nine sweetie-pies yesterday. *Nine!* Pink-striped, green-striped, purple-striped . . .'

Jessie knew that there was no way she was going to make the fairies leave now. Frowning slightly, she closed the door in the hedge behind her and began walking up toward the house. For the first time in her life, she felt annoyed with her beloved grandmother.

Why has Granny put treats for the fairies in the secret garden? she thought crossly. *Doesn't she realise that it's risky to encourage them to come here too often just now?*

No, she doesn't! Jessie stopped suddenly as the thought struck her.

Granny had lived at Blue Moon for over fifty years—ever since she had left her life as a princess of the Realm to marry Robert Belairs, the human man she loved. For all that time the Blue Moon garden had been safe for any fairy, pixie, or other magical creature who had cared to visit.

But Granny had been away for two whole weeks, because the long-awaited exhibition of Robert Belairs's fairy paintings had begun at the National Gallery. The real trouble hadn't started till after she left.

Granny didn't know just how much of a pest Mrs Tweedie had become. She didn't know that the woman was not only prying in the house, but had started making endless, feeble excuses for prowling around the Blue Moon garden.

Oh, I wish Mrs Tweedie had never come here! Jessie thought angrily as she started hurrying toward the house again. Why did the Bins family have to rent their house to *her*?

The Bins family had been awful neighbours, but at least they'd kept away from Blue Moon. In fact, most of the time they'd tried to pretend that the house, and its unusual owner, just didn't exist. Until that last, terrible day when they'd found out just how unusual Jessie's grandmother was.

Luckily, no-one had believed their terrified babblings of fairy queens and unicorns. Everyone thought they'd lost their minds. After that, they'd fled to the city, and no-one in the mountains had seen them since.

Jessie had been very happy to see them go. It had never occurred to her that the person who came to live in the house after them might be even worse.

Jessie trudged on, glaring through the gaps in the trees at the house next door. It wouldn't have surprised her to see a red-tipped nose poking over the fence, or a pair of sharp eyes peering from one of the windows.

'Poor Louise.' Jessie's mother had laughed, when Jessie had complained about Mrs Tweedie. 'She's just lonely. What does it matter if she wanders around in here? It's not as if we have anything to hide.'

But we do, Mum, Jessie had thought desperately. You just don't know it. And for the millionth time, she'd wished her mother *did* know about the Realm, and the secret Door at the bottom of the Blue Moon garden.

'There are Doors to the Realm all over the world, Jessie,' her grandmother had told her. 'But only people who believe in magic can find them. That's what keeps them safe. Everyone has to discover the Realm for himself or herself. As you did, when you first came to live here—and as my Robert did, long ago.'

But Rosemary had spent her childhood at Blue Moon. How could it be that she'd never seen a fairy, pixie, or elf in all that time?

She probably *did* see them, actually, Jessie thought, as she reached the back door and pulled it open. She just didn't realise what they were. Mum doesn't believe in fairies—Granny said she never did, even when she was little. She didn't expect to see fairies, and so she didn't. If she caught sight of them out of the corner of her eye, she thought they were butterflies, or shadows, or leaves blowing in the wind.

And Rosemary had never suspected, as she watched her father painting the fairyland pictures that had made him famous, that he was painting things he'd really seen. Like everyone else, she just thought he had a wonderful imagination.

Jessie went into the warm kitchen and pulled off her jacket. She was just about to call her mother when she heard the sound of voices drifting from the living room. She groaned silently. So Mrs Tweedie hadn't been able to do without her daily visit after all!

She thought of going outside again, then decided to tiptoe to her room instead. She crept into the hallway, trying not to make the old boards creak.

'It was very good of you to take the trouble to come,' Jessie heard her mother say from the living room.

'It was no trouble,' a cool voice answered. 'I've been wanting to talk to you about this for a while. Then I heard that the Open Day was tomorrow, so naturally . . .'

Jessie froze. That wasn't Mrs Tweedie's voice. It belonged to the person who was the second biggest problem in her life—her school teacher, Ms Stone.

CHAPTER TWO

Unwelcome Guests

hy is old Stoneface here? Jessie thought
in panic. I haven't done anything to annoy her
lately. Well, except reading that book about pixies
in reading time on Friday. But L.T. Bowers is a well-
known writer, and I did get the book out of the
library. And I haven't written any fairy stories for
ages, or talked about fairy things, or . . .

'I'll think carefully about what you've said, Lyn,'
said Rosemary. 'Of course, I'm delighted that you
think Jessie's so talented. But—'

'Naturally it's a difficult decision for you,' Ms Stone
broke in smoothly. 'But you have Jessica's future to
think about. A city school like Marchbanks that

specialises in guiding talented students is just what she needs.'

Jessie's stomach turned over. She pressed her hand to her mouth, listening intently.

'Houses and flats are expensive in the city, I know,' she heard Ms Stone say. 'Still, sacrifices have to be made if—'

'Actually, I didn't sell our city house when we came here,' Rosemary said quietly. 'It's rented, at the moment. I haven't been able to make up my mind to sell, just in case . . . But, the thing is, Lyn, Jessie loves living here, at Blue Moon. She's very close to her grandmother, and—'

'If you'll forgive me for saying so, Rosemary, I think that's half the trouble,' Ms Stone interrupted. 'Because you go out to work, Jessica spends a lot of time alone with Mrs Belairs. Isn't that so?'

'Well, yes,' said Rosemary, sounding a bit bewildered. 'But—'

'I have never met Mrs Belairs,' Ms Stone said. 'But Jessica's fascination with old-fashioned fairy stories and fantasy clearly shows her grandmother's influence. Frankly, it's the worst influence in the world for her. She's reading all sorts of rubbish— fiction that pretends to be fact. And she's not developing her writing talent as she should.'

Jessie's face was burning. She wanted to run in there, shouting to her mother not to listen, not to believe a word Ms Stone was saying. But then she'd have to admit she'd been lurking in the hallway, listening.

'Well, I'll leave you to think about it,' said Ms Stone. 'But do try to get to the Marchbanks Open Day tomorrow. I'm sure you'll be very impressed.'

There was the sound of movement, as though she was rising to her feet. Jessie darted back to the kitchen, out of sight.

'Thank you again, Lyn,' she heard her mother say, as the front door opened. 'You're very good to take such an interest in Jessie.'

'She reminds me of myself as a child,' said Ms Stone abruptly. 'Intelligent but dreamy, with no control over her imagination. Her mind is cluttered with useless fancies—as mine was, for a long, long time.'

Jessie listened, fascinated. She found it hard to imagine cool, confident Lyn Stone being a child—let alone a dreamy one. In the classroom, Ms Stone was interested in nothing but facts, facts, facts.

'My foster parents were good people, but they didn't understand me at all,' Ms Stone said. 'For a while they tried to make me focus on practical things. Then they just gave up and let me dream my childhood away.'

'I suppose they thought it was best not to push you,' said Rosemary.

'I suppose so,' Ms Stone agreed coolly. 'But the result was that I grew up feeling a stranger in the real world. I couldn't tell fact from fantasy, and I couldn't cope with real-life problems. My foster parents died when I was in my teens, and after that, life became very hard for me. I was difficult and lonely. I had trouble making friends. I survived, but it wasn't easy.'

Her voice hardened. 'As a teacher, I'm determined not to let any child in my care go through what I did, if I can prevent it. That's why I refuse to allow fantasy in my classroom. And that's why I'm here today.'

'I understand,' Rosemary said. Her voice was serious and rather sad.

'A school like Marchbanks would have been the best thing that had ever happened to me,' Ms Stone said flatly. 'Just as, in my opinion, it would be the best thing for Jessica.'

Jessie groped her way to the back door and silently let herself out. She sat on the step, taking great gulps of fresh, cool air, trying to calm down.

Mum won't take me away to some special school just because Ms Stone says so, she told herself. Mum knows that I'm not like Ms Stone was. *I have friends. I can handle real-life problems.*

But Ms Stone had been so earnest, and so convincing! And Rosemary had sounded very serious and sad, as if she'd begun to think Ms Stone might be right.

Jessie heard the sound of a car starting up at the front of the house. Ms Stone was leaving. Jessie got to her feet and went back into the house, shutting the door loudly behind her.

'Jessie, is that you?' she heard her mother call.

'Yes,' Jessie called back.

Rosemary came into the kitchen. Without a word, she crossed the room and put her arms around Jessie, hugging her tightly.

'Is something wrong, Mum?' asked Jessie. She held her breath, waiting for Rosemary to tell her about Ms Stone's visit.

'Of course not,' said Rosemary, standing back and forcing a smile. 'I was just thinking—how grown-up you're getting. I'll make us some lunch. What do you feel like?'

She went to the refrigerator and looked inside. 'It might be better for you to go to Sal's for the day, tomorrow, instead of coming with me to the airport to pick up Granny,' she said, without turning around. 'I've decided to leave here very early. There are a few things I'd like to do before I go to the airport.'

Like go to the Marchbanks Open Day, Jessie thought dismally. Oh, Mum!

There was a light tap on the back door. 'Yoo-hoo, it's only me!' called Mrs Tweedie, sounding far less chirpy than usual.

Rosemary sighed and turned away from the fridge. 'Come in, Louise,' she called back.

Mrs Tweedie tottered into the kitchen, a wad of tissues held to her nose and tears streaming from her puffy, red-rimmed eyes. 'It's the fumes from the new paint,' she snuffled, before anyone could ask her what was wrong. 'I'm always sensitive to things like that. But I didn't like to object when Mr Bins said the house had to be painted.'

'Oh, what a nuisance for you, Louise,' said Rosemary, looking concerned.

Mrs Tweedie sank into a chair and hunched there, sniffing dolefully. Her spiky hair was ruffled. She looked like a bedraggled hen.

She smells like one, too, Jessie thought, wrinkling her nose. Or she smells of something. She's rubbed some stuff on her chest to unblock her nose, I suppose.

'I don't know what I'm going to do,' Mrs Tweedie moaned, putting her head in her hands. 'I can't stay in that house, but I've got nowhere else to go.'

Jessie glanced urgently at her mother. Don't ask her here, she begged silently. Don't ask her . . .

'I rang Mr Bins, but he just said I should move into a hotel for a couple of days,' sniffed Mrs Tweedie. 'He doesn't seem to understand that I can't possibly afford—'

'Louise, don't be silly,' said Rosemary, frowning at Jessie, who was mouthing 'No! No!' and shaking her head. 'You can stay here. We've got a spare room.'

Mrs Tweedie lifted her head, and Jessie was sure she saw a spark of triumph in the watery, red-rimmed eyes.

'Oh, that would be wonderful!' Mrs Tweedie gasped. Then she clasped her hands anxiously. 'But your mother gets home tomorrow afternoon, doesn't she, Rosemary? And you and Jessie are going down to pick her up? You'll all be very tired when you get home. You won't want a stranger—'

'It won't be any trouble at all, Louise,' Rosemary broke in firmly. 'Mum will be pleased to see you. I'm just sorry you'll have to spend the day on your own.'

Jessie took a deep breath. 'Mum,' she said, 'if Mrs Tweedie is going to be here, then I can stay here, too, can't I? I mean, I don't need to go to Sal's at all.'

Rosemary's eyes widened. She couldn't understand why Jessie would want to spend the day with Mrs Tweedie. And Jessie *didn't* want to—not at all. But she wanted to leave Mrs Tweedie alone at Blue Moon even less.

'Jessie's not going with me,' Rosemary explained to Mrs Tweedie, who was also looking surprised. 'She was going to spend the day with a friend. But—'

'Oh, you mustn't change your plans for *me*, Jessie,' Mrs Tweedie exclaimed. 'That really *would* upset me.'

'It's okay,' Jessie said sweetly. 'I've—I've got lots of homework to do, anyway. I'd really rather stay home.'

A trace of annoyance crossed Mrs Tweedie's face. It disappeared instantly, but Jessie had seen it.

Got you! she thought with grim satisfaction. You thought your chance had come, didn't you? You thought you'd have a whole day to prowl around Blue Moon and sticky-beak everywhere with no-one to see what you were doing. Well, too bad. I'm staying.

CHAPTER THREE

Suspicion

n ten minutes, Mrs Tweedie had moved into the small spare bedroom across the hall from Jessie's room. Rosemary found some clean sheets, while Jessie carried in Mrs Tweedie's neat little overnight bag, which was surprisingly heavy. Mrs Tweedie thanked them over and over again, then insisted they leave her to settle in. Gratefully, Jessie and Rosemary escaped to the kitchen. It was such a relief to get away from her constant talking.

'Her bag was already packed, Mum,' Jessie whispered as her mother began chopping onions to make soup for dinner. 'She *knew* you'd ask her to stay.'

'Of course she did,' Rosemary whispered back,

blinking as the onion began to make her eyes water. 'But that doesn't make any difference. You could see for yourself what the paint fumes had done to her. The poor thing was—'

'Oh!' Jessie squealed.

Rosemary jumped in shock, nearly dropping the knife. 'Jessie, I almost cut myself!' she exclaimed. 'What's the matter with you?'

'Onion!' Jessie breathed. 'That's what Mrs Tweedie smelled of when she came in—raw onion! Mum, she doesn't have an allergy at all! She used onion to make her eyes water and go red!'

Rosemary sighed and turned back to the chopping board. 'Jessie, you're letting your imagination run away with you,' she said. 'You don't like Mrs Tweedie, but that's no excuse for being mean. The poor woman is here because she didn't have anywhere else to go.'

'Well, if she's so poor, why did she rent the Bins' house?' Jessie snapped back. 'Why didn't she rent something smaller?'

'She probably got a special deal,' Rosemary said, wiping her eyes on her sleeve. 'She knows the Bins family quite well, I think. They rented the flat next door to hers for a while, when they first went back to the city.'

Jessie's jaw dropped. 'Mrs Tweedie lived next door to the *Bins*?' she gasped. 'Does Granny know that?'

'Well, I don't suppose she does,' Rosemary said. 'I'd more or less forgotten about it myself till now. Louise let it slip to me one day. I don't think she meant to because she got very flustered and started rattling on about something else.'

She grinned. 'She was probably embarrassed. She must know we weren't friendly with the Bins family. You can imagine what they said to her about us. Jess, could you go out and get me some parsley, please?'

Jessie almost ran to the back door, escaping from the house with relief. The discovery that Mrs Tweedie actually knew the Bins family had left her breathless.

What *had* the Bins told Mrs Tweedie? What if they'd told her about the strange things they'd seen and heard at Blue Moon? And what if Mrs Tweedie hadn't thought they were crazy? What if she'd believed them?

That would explain a lot. It would explain why, from the very beginning, Mrs Tweedie had been so interested in Blue Moon—and why she was always making excuses to wander around the garden. Poking her sharp, little nose into every hidden corner, peering about with those bright, darting eyes . . .

Jessie knelt down and clumsily picked a small bunch of parsley from the patch near the back door. Her fingers felt stiff. Her heart was thudding wildly. She heard a small, enquiring trill and looked up. Flynn, Granny's big orange cat, was sitting on the grass nearby, watching her.

'I think Mrs Tweedie knows about the Realm, Flynn,' Jessie whispered. 'Or she suspects something, anyway. And now she's actually staying in the house! Granny will be home tomorrow night, and she'll know what to do. But until then we mustn't let Mrs Tweedie out of our sight. Not for a minute.'

'Jessie!'

Jessie looked quickly around. Her mother was standing at the back door with her hands on her hips. 'Jessie, I'm waiting for that parsley!' Rosemary exclaimed. 'What are you doing crouched there, talking to yourself?'

'Oh, sorry!' gabbled Jessie, scrambling to her feet. 'But I wasn't talking to myself. I was talking to Flynn.'

'Oh, really?' said Rosemary dryly. 'You're getting as bad as your grandmother.' She turned and went back into the house.

Jessie followed miserably. Her worry about Mrs Tweedie had made her forget Ms Stone's visit for a while. Now the memory of it returned in full force.

Oh, why had she said she'd been talking to Flynn? It seemed that everything she did gave her mother even more reason to think that the sooner she was away from Granny, the better.

Rosemary left early the next morning. Before she went, she urged Jessie to go to Sal's for the day as planned. 'You and Sal are still good friends, aren't you?' she asked, a little anxiously.

'Of course we are!' said Jessie, the memory of Ms Stone's remarks about friends very clear in her mind. 'I just don't want to leave Mrs Tweedie here on her own.'

Rosemary took a breath to say something, then changed her mind and shook her head helplessly instead.

Jessie waved until the car was out of sight. Then, sick at heart, she returned to the kitchen. It didn't improve her mood to find Mrs Tweedie, in a smart cherry-red dressing gown and matching slippers, standing at the kitchen bench, making coffee.

Flynn was crouched by the door, watching Mrs Tweedie with slitted eyes. He looked half asleep, but Jessie knew he was fully alert, keeping his part of their bargain.

'Good morning, dear,' Mrs Tweedie chirped, replacing the lid on a tin of strong-smelling coffee she'd obviously brought from home.

'Are you feeling better today, Mrs Tweedie?' Jessie asked.

'Oh, yes,' Mrs Tweedie said brightly. 'Now that I'm away from that awful paint I'm feeling almost as good as new.'

In fact, she looked even better than new, Jessie thought. The red dressing gown suited her much better than the dowdy, old-lady clothes she usually wore. Her eyes were clear and sparkling. Even her movements, as she poured her coffee and sat down at the table were firmer and less fussy than usual. It was as if she'd become years younger overnight.

'I'd be *quite* all right on my own today, you know,' said Mrs Tweedie, looking up at Jessie over the rim of her coffee cup. 'Are you sure you don't want to go to Sal's after all?'

'Oh, no,' Jessie answered lightly. 'I'm fine here, really.'

Again she saw a flash of anger in the bright bird's eyes. Then the eyes dropped, and for a few minutes Mrs Tweedie sat in silence, drinking her coffee thoughtfully.

This is like a game of chess, Jessie said to herself. What's her next move going to be?

The next move was unexpected. Mrs Tweedie stood up, put her coffee cup on the sink, and announced that she was going to have a nice, quiet day. Then she simply went to her room and shut the door behind her.

Jessie spent the next few hours in her own room, trying to read her library book, but finding it very hard to concentrate. The book had some fuzzy-looking black and white pictures that showed what were supposed to be pixies, photographed in secret. The pixies could have been anything from toadstools to cardboard cut-outs, but L.T. Bowers seemed to have no doubt that they were real.

Restlessly, Jessie turned to the front of the book and read the titles of the other books L.T. Bowers had written. *Haunted Houses of the World*, she read. *Bigfoot: Fact or Fable? . . . The Loch Ness Monster . . .*

Her attention wandered. Her door was wide open, and the spare room was right across the hall. She'd know at once if Mrs Tweedie came out. But still she found herself glancing up over and over again.

Maybe I'm being as silly as Mum thinks I am, she thought. Maybe I'm giving myself a miserable, boring Sunday all for nothing. But she turned back to her place and sat stubbornly staring at *Pixies on the Moor*, reading the same sentences over and over again, while the morning slipped away.

At midday, the doorbell rang, making her jump. The spare room door snapped open and Mrs Tweedie appeared, wearing slim black trousers, a white silk shirt, and a red jacket. 'I'll get it,' she chirped, flashing a smile at Jessie. She shut the door behind her and strode quickly away.

Jessie heard her open the front door. She heard the murmur of voices, among them the high, piping voice of a young child. At the same moment, a draught swept down the hallway. The spare room door clicked and swung open, giving Jessie a clear view of Mrs Tweedie's belongings arranged neatly on the old desk that stood beside the bed.

A laptop computer, its screen dark. A very expensive-looking camera. A video camera. A mobile phone.

Jessie's eyes widened. She didn't know exactly how much all these things cost, but she did know that they weren't the possessions of someone who was as short of money as Mrs Tweedie claimed to be.

Neither is that red dressing gown, she thought suddenly. Or even the coffee. Mrs Tweedie isn't poor! She just pretends she is.

Just like she pretends she's just a fussy, harmless old duck, a voice in her mind added, when really she's nothing of the kind.

A tingling feeling ran down Jessie's spine.

CHAPTER FOUR

Tasha

The front door closed, but Mrs Tweedie was still talking. Realising that someone had come in, Jessie put her book down and hurried out of her room.

At the kitchen door she met Mrs Tweedie and a wide-eyed little girl of about four. The girl was wearing pink overalls, a pink-and-white-striped top, and a pair of silver fairy wings. A gauzy butterfly was clipped to her short, black curls. She was clutching a battered blue rabbit.

'Ah, there you are, Jessie,' said Mrs Tweedie, in a falsely sweet voice. 'This is my little friend, Tasha. Tasha and Bunny have come to visit me, while their mummy goes to work. Isn't that lovely?'

'Oh—yes,' Jessie stammered. Tasha put her finger in her mouth and crushed the blue rabbit more tightly to her chest.

'Do you know, yesterday I'd quite forgotten that Tasha was coming today?' Mrs Tweedie went on, still in that awful, fake voice. 'Then, this morning I remembered. So I rang Tasha's mummy and told her that my house is full of nasty paint smells, so Tasha could visit me here, instead.'

Tasha took her finger out of her mouth. 'In the fairy house,' she said.

'That's right!' said Mrs Tweedie, glancing quickly at Jessie. 'Now, Tasha, would you like an ice-cream? You like ice-cream, don't you?'

'Yes!' said Tasha, her face breaking into a smile. 'With chockie on.'

'You ask Jessie if she'll go to the shops and buy us all a chocolate-coated ice-cream, then,' said Mrs Tweedie. 'Ask her very, very nicely. Say, "*Please*, Jessie!"'

'*Please*, Jessie!' Tasha repeated, her face glowing.

'Pretty please,' cooed Mrs Tweedie, handing Jessie some money.

Jessie didn't want to go anywhere, but she knew she had no choice. She just couldn't say no to the little girl who was looking up at her so trustingly.

And Mrs Tweedie knows it, too, she thought angrily, as she left the house and hurried up the street. She's got rid of me at last.

She found that she was almost running, and forced herself to slow down. Don't be stupid, she told herself sternly. You'll be away only half an hour. Anyway, Mrs Tweedie won't be able to do much spying with a four year old trailing around after her, watching everything she does. She'd be too scared of Tasha talking about it to me afterward.

Still, she fretted as she made her long way to the shops, waited to be served, and jogged home again. She knew she wouldn't be happy until she had Mrs Tweedie safely under her eye again.

❦

The house was quiet when Jessie got home. Even Flynn was nowhere to be seen.

'Hello!' Jessie called, thrusting the melting ice-creams into the freezer. 'Mrs Tweedie? Tasha?'

Then she saw the note on the kitchen table. The writing was Mrs Tweedie's, but it was scrawled, as though it had been written in a rush.

Jessie—

Tasha is missing. I only turned my back for a minute, and she was gone. She's nowhere in the house or garden. Might have tried to walk home. I'm going out to look for her.

Mrs T.

Jessie stared at the note, a hot tide of anger washing over her. Only turned your back for a minute, did you? she thought furiously. Oh, sure! I'll bet you nipped off to sticky-beak in Grandpa's studio as soon as I'd gone and left Tasha by herself. How could you be so stupid?

The anger was quickly replaced by fear, as she thought of a four year old walking the streets alone. Did Tasha even *know* her way home from Blue Moon? What if she'd wandered into the bush at the end of the street? How long had she been missing? Ten minutes? Twenty?

Flynn! she thought suddenly. Where's Flynn? He might know where Tasha is.

She bolted through the back door, almost colliding with a bald man in paint-smeared white overalls who was standing on the back step, with his hand raised to knock.

'Oh, sorry, love,' the man said. 'Mrs Tweedie there?'

'Have you seen a little dark-haired girl anywhere?' Jessie gasped. 'A four-year-old girl? Carrying a blue rabbit? Wearing a pink—'

'Nope,' the man said. 'Haven't seen her, sorry. Look, I need a word with Mrs Tweedie.'

'She's not here,' said Jessie. 'She's gone to—'

'Strike me lucky,' the man said, his forehead wrinkling all the way up to his bald scalp. 'She lays it on us to work this weekend, says it's *got* to be this weekend—though it beats me why it's so urgent when the old paint's still good as new and she's not even changing the colour. Then she goes off and leaves us flat!'

He turned away. 'You just tell her we're painting the bedroom cupboards same as the doors, then, will you love?' he said. 'Double pay or no double pay, we can't hang around waiting. Got to start another job Monday.'

He slouched off, shaking his head and muttering to himself. Jessie stared after him in confusion. He'd talked as if Mrs Tweedie had organised the painting of the house herself, but the painting was all Mr Bins' doing.

Or *was* it? They only had Mrs Tweedie's word for it. And the more Jessie thought about what the painter had said, the more she doubted that Mrs

Tweedie had been telling the truth. There was no way Mr Bins would spend money on having his house painted if it didn't need it. And there was no way he'd pay double to get the job done on one particular weekend, either.

So . . . Mrs Tweedie had lied. *She* had brought the painters in. *She* had wanted the job done this weekend—and she was paying a lot for it. But why?

'Could it possibly be because Mum and I were going to the city today, to pick up Granny?' Jessie whispered aloud. 'Could she possibly have planned the whole thing just so that she could have Blue Moon to herself for once?'

She shook her head violently. No. That was ridiculous. She was letting her imagination run away with her, just as her mother had said. Just as Ms Stone always said, too.

And it didn't even matter, really. If Mrs Tweedie *had* made some weird, elaborate plan to give herself a day alone at Blue Moon, her plan had been ruined—first by Jessie's staying home, then by Tasha's coming to stay.

Tasha! Jessie realised that she'd completely forgotten about poor little Tasha.

'Flynn!' she shouted at the top of her voice. 'Where are you, Flynn?'

As if in answer, there was a tremendous crash from the shed behind the garage at the side of the house.

Jessie ran to the shed. She could see nothing through the tiny window, but yowls of rage were coming from behind the door, which was bolted shut. Jessie wrestled with the heavy bolt and finally managed to pull it free. She dragged the sagging door open.

Flynn streaked out of the dimness, his orange fur standing on end, his green eyes blazing with fury. The floor of the shed was littered with the smashed remains of the pots he'd pushed off a shelf to attract her attention.

'Flynn! How did you get in there?' Jessie gasped. 'Did you follow Mrs Tweedie in, while she was looking for Tasha? Did you get locked in by mistake? Flynn, could you see anything through the window? Do you know where Tasha is?'

Flynn made a furious, huffing sound and raced off through the trees. Jessie's stomach turned over as she saw that he was heading for the secret garden. She ran after him.

The door in the hedge was half open. Flynn ran through the gap. Jessie followed, her heart thudding.

The secret garden was deserted, but something with gauzy pink wings gleamed on the smooth green grass. For a moment Jessie thought it was a real butterfly. Then she realised that it was Tasha's hair clip.

'She's been here, all right,' Jessie beathed, picking up the clip. 'But—where did she go after that? She's only little. She wouldn't have been able to walk all the way back up to the street from here, and disappear before Mrs Tweedie started looking for her. Where is she?'

Flynn trilled impatiently. He stared at Jessie fixedly, his tail lashing, as though she was being very stupid.

And Jessie's heart lurched. She remembered Tasha's silver fairy wings. Her grandmother's voice echoed in her mind.

There are Doors to the Realm all over the world, Jessie. But only people who believe in magic can find them.

'Tasha found the Door!' Jessie heard herself saying. 'She—she's gone into the Realm! Oh, Flynn!'

Flynn miaowed urgently.

Jessie knew what she had to do. She pushed Tasha's hair clip deep into her pocket. 'Open!' she called, and felt herself being swept away.

The next moment, she was blinking in the soft sunlight of the Realm. Quickly she looked around, but there was no sign of Tasha. In fact, there was no-one to be seen at all. The pebbly road stretched away to left and right, bare and empty. No white rabbits nibbled the sweet grass beyond. No fairies flitted among the trees.

Jessie called Tasha's name, but there was no answer. Trying not to panic, she realised that by now the little girl might have wandered too far from the Door to hear her. Which way had she gone? Her small feet had left no traces on the pebbles of the road, or on the grass.

'Where are you, Tasha?' Jessie shouted. An aching lump rose in her throat. Tears burned in her eyes.

Stop it! she told herself furiously, fighting back the tears. It's no use standing here blubbering. You've got to get help!

She ran for the palace. By the time she reached it she was gasping for breath and her side was aching, but she didn't stop. She raced down the side of the great golden building till she reached Patrice's door. She pounded on the door with her fists.

For an awful moment she thought there was no-one home. Then, with a wave of relief, she heard the sound of hurrying footsteps from inside the little housekeeper's apartment.

'No need to break it down!' shrieked Patrice, throwing the door open with a scowl. 'What in the Realm do you think . . .? Jessie!'

Her frown turned into a look of amazement as Jessie almost fell through the door into her arms.

'Oh—Patrice!' Jessie gasped, and burst into tears.

'Maybelle!' Patrice shrieked. 'Giff! Come quickly!'

CHAPTER FIVE

The Rainbow Wand

In moments, Jessie was sitting in Patrice's cosy kitchen and a glass of cool water was being pressed into her hand. Patrice, Maybelle, and Giff huddled around her as, between sobs, she poured out her story.

'Don't cry, Jessie,' wailed Giff, whose own eyes had filled with tears at the sight of Jessie's distress. 'You don't have to worry about Tasha. All little children are safe in the Realm.'

'That's right, dearie,' said Patrice gently. 'The real dangers—star fairies and Peskies and things like that—are far away from the Doors. Human children who find their way into the Realm are always looked after. They always meet some fairies, or a miniature horse or an elf or someone who'll help them home when it's time.'

Maybelle snorted. 'Jessie knows that!' she snapped. 'That's not the problem. Didn't you hear what she said? That Tweedie woman thinks the little human's lost! She's rushing around trying to find her! She'll have police swarming all over the Blue Moon garden next. It's dangerous, Patrice!'

Giff whimpered, and Patrice's round face clouded. 'I hadn't thought of that,' she admitted slowly. She turned to Jessie. 'Do these police people believe in magic, dearie?' she asked.

Jessie wiped her eyes. 'Some of them might,' she managed to say. 'And, Patrice, if just one gets through the Door, all the others would see! And then—'

'Word would spread,' Maybelle said grimly, lashing her tail.

'The newspapers and TV people would hear about it,' said Jessie. 'In a few days Blue Moon would be crawling with people trying to—'

'No-one who means harm can enter the Realm while the magic's strong,' Patrice said stoutly.

'Maybe not,' growled Maybelle. 'But we aren't just talking about people who actually mean harm here, Patrice! We're talking about ordinary, curious humans—thousands of them—flooding into the Realm! Queen Helena would have to lock the Blue Moon Door to stop them. But one by one the other Doors would be found, too. And in the end—well, in the end, we'd have to cut ourselves off from the human world forever.'

She glanced at Jessie. 'That's what you're afraid of, Jessie, isn't it?' she asked bluntly.

Jessie nodded, unable to speak.

Patrice pursed her lips. 'Well, we'd better find the little girl as quickly as we can, then, and get her home,' she said. 'The guards can spread the word to everyone within walking distance of the Door— fairies, water sprites, Folk, horses, elves, pixies, unicorns—even the rabbits. Tasha can't have got far. Someone will find her.'

She bustled out of the kitchen and disappeared through the door that led into the palace.

'Of course she'll be found in the end, but it'll take time,' said Maybelle, tapping a hoof restlessly. 'And time is what we don't have if we're going to stop that Tweedie woman from panicking. The girl could be anywhere! If only we knew which way she'd gone.'

'The Rainbow Wand could tell us,' Giff said suddenly.

Maybelle's hoof stopped tapping. Jessie seized Giff's arm. 'What's the Rainbow Wand?' she asked eagerly.

Giff looked startled. 'It's . . . um . . . it's a magic wand that finds lost people,' he said. 'But—'

'Oh, look what you've done, you fool of an elf!' Maybelle shouted, as Jessie jumped to her feet in excitement. 'You've got her all fired up now. And you *know* Avron won't let us have the Rainbow Wand!'

'I was just saying—' Giff wailed.

'What's all the shouting about?' scolded Patrice, hurrying back into the room. 'Giff! Maybelle! Can't I leave you for five minutes without—'

'Patrice!' exclaimed Jessie. 'Giff's just told me about the Rainbow Wand! Who is Avron? Where can I find him?'

Patrice's plump face went blank. 'The—the Rainbow Wand,' she said slowly. 'Oh, dearie, we can't—'

'I know that for some reason Avron keeps the Rainbow Wand to himself and won't let anyone else use it,' Jessie broke in fiercely. 'But this time he'll have to change his mind. It's important to the whole Realm! Where does he live? Is it far away?'

'No,' said Patrice, smoothing her skirt nervously.

'Avron lives in one of the palace towers. But—'

'Then take me to him,' Jessie said, almost jumping out of her skin with impatience. 'I'll talk to him. I'll *make* him give us the Wand. I'll tell him—tell him Granny wants him to lend it to us. Surely he'd listen then.'

Patrice glanced at Maybelle, who had started tapping her hoof again. 'We could give it a try, Maybelle,' Patrice said. 'It can't do any harm to try.'

'Oh, no harm at all!' snapped Maybelle. 'Getting hit by a thunderbolt or being turned into furry caterpillars will just be a little bit of fun for us, won't it?'

Giff gave a terrified shriek and clapped his hand over his mouth.

Patrice snorted. 'Avron had better not try any funny business like that with me,' she said crossly. 'I've known him since he was in baby robes. I'll take Jessie to the tower by the back way. If you don't want to come with us, then don't!'

Seizing Jessie's arm, she hurried her out of the kitchen and through the door that led to the rest of the palace. 'They'll come,' she muttered grimly, as she and Jessie began to hurry along a deserted corridor.

Jessie looked over her shoulder. Sure enough, far behind her, the door to Patrice's apartment was slowly swinging open again, and Maybelle and Giff were coming out.

'Who *is* Avron, Patrice?' she asked, as the little housekeeper darted up a steep flight of steps. 'Why are you all so scared of him?'

'Avron is—or was—the Realm's most brilliant magician,' Patrice panted, reaching the top of the steps and beginning to trot along another corridor. 'He created hundreds of wonders in his time—the Ribbon Roads, for example.'

'And the Rainbow Wand?' Jessie asked quickly.

'Yes,' said Patrice. 'The Rainbow Wand was his last invention—the one that ruined his life and ended his career.' Before Jessie could ask what she meant, she pointed to a door just ahead. 'That door leads into Avron's tower,' she said. 'There's no lock on it—no need for one. Folk know to keep away.'

When they reached the door, Patrice leaned against the wall beside it, fanning herself. 'I need a minute to catch my breath,' she gasped. 'We've got another steep climb ahead of us. Avron's rooms are right at the top of the tower.'

Jessie heard the clip-clopping of small hoofs. She turned quickly to see Maybelle and Giff coming down the corridor toward them, looking hot and fearful. 'Will Avron really try to hurt us, or—or change us into anything?' she asked, thinking nervously of Maybelle's warning.

Patrice wiped her damp forehead. 'He might,' she admitted. 'I'm hoping he'll listen to what you have to say before he acts, but he's angry and bitter enough to do anything. For twenty-five years the Tower of Avron has been forbidden to everyone— even Queen Helena. Avron speaks to no-one.'

'But why, Patrice?' Jessie exclaimed. 'And why did you say the Rainbow Wand ruined his life?'

'Avron had a child,' Patrice said quietly. 'Her name was Linnet. Her mother died just after she was born, so she was all Avron had. She was an enchanting little thing—I remember her well, laughing and playing around the palace. Everyone loved her, and as for Avron—well, Linnet was the light of his life. Then—he lost her.'

'*Lost* her?' said Jessie. 'You mean Linnet died too?'

'No,' said Patrice. 'Twenty-five years ago, Linnet just—disappeared.'

The Tower of Avron

s Jessie stared, Patrice bit her lip. 'Avron was travelling around the Realm with Linnet,' she said. 'He was using her to test the Rainbow Wand. He'd ask her to hide from him, in the cleverest places she could think of, and then he'd use the Wand to find her. But one day, while they were in the north . . .'

'One day he *couldn't* find her,' Jessie whispered.

Patrice nodded, her round face filled with sorrow. 'The Rainbow Wand led Avron to a Door on the Realm's northern border. That Door is hardly ever used, because it leads to a busy street in the heart of a human city. Avron realised that Linnet had tried to trick him properly by going into your world. It had never occurred to him that she might do that. She'd never been outside the Realm in her life.'

She sighed. 'Avron went through the Door himself, of course, but he couldn't find Linnet. Like a lot of magic, the Rainbow Wand doesn't work as strongly in your world as it does in the Realm. It would have sensed Linnet if she'd stayed beside the Door, but she'd wandered away, and of course she'd got lost. She was a bright little girl, but very young—no older than your Tasha.'

She shook her head. 'Avron searched frantically for months, but it was as if Linnet had disappeared into thin air. At last even he had to admit the search was hopeless. He retreated to his tower and there he's stayed for twenty-five years, alone with his grief. And Linnet has never been seen again.'

'That's so—so terrible, Patrice!' Jessie whispered.

Patrice nodded sadly. 'Linnet isn't the first of our children to be lost in your world, dearie, and I don't suppose she'll be the last,' she murmured. 'If Realm Folk stay too long in your world, their memories fade very quickly. Well, you know that—it's why your grandmother always wears her charm bracelet, to keep her memories of the Realm fresh.'

Jessie looked down at her own bracelet. Every one of its charms had been a gift from the Realm. Every one had a story to tell. So far, all the stories had ended happily. But how would this story end?

'It could end with Blue Moon being invaded by thousands of people, and the Realm being cut off from the mortal world forever,' she said aloud. 'But not if I can find Tasha quickly. Not if I can get the Rainbow Wand.'

She looked up and saw Patrice staring at her helplessly. 'Come on, Patrice,' she said abruptly. 'I can't wait a minute longer.'

She pulled the tower door open and stepped into the dimness beyond. Before Patrice could follow, the door swung shut again, closing with a loud click.

Startled, Jessie spun around. The doorknob was rattling, twisting uselessly this way and that. 'Jessie!' Patrice shrieked, her muffled voice high with panic. 'I can't get the door open! Can you do it from your side?'

Jessie tried her best, but the door remained firmly closed. She felt something touch her cheek—something cool, soft, and slightly sticky. She jumped and tried to brush the thing away. It clung to her hand and she saw that it was a thick white thread, like a strand of web spun by a giant spider.

Shuddering, Jessie tore her hand free and turned, flattening her back against the door.

Now that her eyes had adjusted to the dimness, she could see that she was in a tall, echoing space with rounded walls. A steep, golden staircase wound up through the centre of the space, disappearing into darkness at the top. And hanging all around the staircase, trailing down from the darkness to the floor, were hundreds of the thick white threads.

Jessie shrank back, her heart thudding wildly. Dimly she could hear Patrice, Maybelle and Giff hitting and kicking the door, but her eyes were fixed on the white threads. They were drifting toward her, swaying closer with every breath she took. Every thread was quivering as if it were alive.

Then she was caught. One moment she was pressed hard against the door. The next moment, the mass of soft, sticky threads had surged against her, wound around her and jerked her off her feet.

Struggling and screaming, Jessie felt herself being dragged upward. The winding staircase was a golden blur beside her as the threads pulled her up, up through echoing space, like a fish caught in a net. She screwed her eyes tightly shut, her breath was sobbing in her throat . . .

Then, abruptly, the dizzying upward rush stopped.

Jessie felt herself thud onto something firm and warm. She lay, trembling and panting, only dimly aware that the threads that bound her were slipping away.

'Who is this, who has dared to invade my tower?'

The voice was deep and harsh. Jessie opened her eyes. She was lying on the carpeted floor of a round room lined with books. Light streamed from tall windows, and through the windows she could see the clear blue of the sky.

A tall man in a shining, dark blue robe was looming over her. His proud face, with its pointed black beard and slanting black eyebrows, was deeply marked with lines of bitterness and grief. Jessie knew that this was Avron.

She struggled to sit up. 'I am Jessie, the granddaughter of Queen Jessica,' she said, in a voice that was little more than a squeak. 'I have come—'

'I know why you have come,' the man said coldly. 'The threads that carried you here are my ears as well as my protection. Through them I hear every word that is said outside my walls. You have come to ask me to lend you the Rainbow Wand. And I tell you now that I will not.'

'But you must!' Jessie cried, staggering to her feet. 'Oh, Avron, you *must*!'

Avron's slanting brows drew together. 'It is unwise to use the word "must" to me, girl,' he hissed. 'Did you not listen to your friend, Patrice? Do you not know my power?'

Jessie felt a thrill of fear. It took all her strength to stop herself from backing away. She swallowed and lifted her chin. 'I am sorry,' she said, trying to keep her voice from trembling. 'It's just—so important that Tasha is found quickly. If she's not—'

Avron's thin lips curved in a bitter smile. 'If she is not, the Realm will be overrun by curious humans,' he said. 'What difference will that make to me? I have already lost everything that gave my life meaning. What do I care what happens now?'

Jessie felt a hot flare of anger. '*You* might not care,' she exclaimed passionately. 'But everyone else in the Realm does. And my grandmother does. And I do. And Linnet would have cared, too. You know she would!'

As soon as she spoke, she knew she had gone too far, but it was too late to take the hasty words back. Avron's face had twisted with rage. His eyes burned like blue fire. He raised his hand. The floor beneath

Jessie's feet trembled. Her skin prickled. The very air of the tower room seemed to quiver.

Jessie shrank back, covering her eyes, waiting in terror for Avron's fury to burst over her.

But nothing happened. Slowly Jessie's skin stopped prickling, and the room fell silent. Fearfully, she let her hands slide away from her eyes. Avron was standing quite still, his arms hanging loosely by his sides. The anger had drained from his face, leaving a terrible sorrow in its place.

'I'm so sorry,' Jessie whispered. 'I shouldn't have said that—about Linnet. It was a terrible thing to do.'

'No,' Avron said in a flat, tired voice. 'You said the words that Linnet would have said, if she had been here to speak for herself. My daughter, like her mother before her, was full of life and laughter. She cared for others. She would have begged me to lend the Rainbow Wand, to save the Realm. And so . . . for her sake . . . I shall.'

The relief was so great that Jessie felt weak at the knees. She clasped her hands to stop them from trembling.

Avron went to a carved wooden chest that stood beneath one of the windows. He lifted the lid of the chest and took something out. When he turned back to Jessie he was holding a plain, polished silver rod.

'This is the Rainbow Wand,' he said curtly. 'It is tuned to find Linnet, and always will be, while I live, but the tuning may be changed for a short time. To do this I need an object belonging to the Lost One.'

'An object . . . ?' For an instant Jessie's heart seemed to stand still. Then she remembered. She pulled the butterfly hair clip from her pocket and held it out.

Avron took the clip and touched it to the tip of the Rainbow Wand, muttering some words that Jessie couldn't hear. The tip of the wand lit with a strange blue glow.

Avron handed the hair clip back to Jessie, then placed the glowing wand in her eager hands. As she began to gasp her thanks, he shook his head. 'Do not thank me yet,' he said gravely. 'You must beware. The Rainbow Wand is very powerful, and it was never truly finished. I put it aside when Linnet was lost.'

He frowned. 'Had I continued with my work, the wand would have been made safe. As it is, it could be dangerous. You must follow my instructions exactly, or you may do more harm with it than good. Do you understand?'

'Yes,' Jessie said breathlessly. 'Yes, Avron. Just tell me what to do.'

CHAPTER SEVEN

The Snairies

Not long afterward, Jessie, Patrice, Maybelle, and Giff were running down the front steps of the Palace.

'Oh, Jessie, I still can't believe you're safe!' Patrice panted. 'When I couldn't open that door I was just so—'

'Stop going on and on about it, Patrice,' Maybelle interrupted impatiently. 'Let's hear what Avron said about the Rainbow Wand.'

'He said that the wand will change colour to show us which way we have to go to find Tasha,' Jessie said. 'If the tip is blue or green—what Avron called *cold* colours—it means we're going the wrong way.

But if the tip turns from yellow to orange to red—
hot colours—it's telling us that we're going the *right*
way.'

'So that's why we came out this way, Jessie,' Giff
said excitedly as they reached the bottom of the
steps. 'Because while you were inside, the wand
went yellow when you pointed it toward the front of
the palace. Oh, that's so clever! Do the colours *feel*
hot and cold?' He stretched out a finger to touch
the glowing tip of the wand.

With a cry of alarm, Jessie jerked it out of his
reach. 'No, Giff!' she gasped. 'It's dangerous for
the wand to touch anyone except the Lost One
it's tuned to find. That's another thing Avron told
me. He's not sure what would happen if the wand
touched someone else, but he thinks there'd be
some sort of explosion, at least.'

Giff snatched his finger back, looking horrified.

'And the brighter the wand is, the more dangerous it is, I suppose,' Patrice asked nervously. 'You'll
be very careful, won't you, Jessie?'

Jessie nodded. 'Don't worry, Patrice,' she said. 'As
soon as I've got Tasha home, I just have to say, "The
Lost One is found!" and the spell will be broken. The
wand will change back to normal, and be safe again.'

'Let's get on with it, then!' snorted Maybelle.

'The sooner we're rid of the thing, the better!'

Jessie held the Rainbow Wand out in front of her and swept it slowly from side to side. The moment it pointed toward the grove of pale-leaved trees that stood at the edge of the grass, the yellow tip brightened and deepened to gold.

'That way!' Maybelle exclaimed in excitement, and Jessie ran, with the Rainbow Wand held high and her friends close behind her.

They threaded their way through the trees, keeping their eyes on the glowing tip of the wand. Jessie waved the wand this way and that as she walked, always moving in the direction that made the golden glow burn brightest.

Soon they were deep inside the grove. The ground was covered in a thick carpet of dead leaves, and their feet made a soft rustling sound as they walked. There was no other noise except the whispering of the trees.

Then Jessie saw something strange hanging from the lowest branch of a tree not far ahead. It was a large, round ball that seemed to be made of twigs and leaves woven together.

She was just about to ask what it was when she heard Patrice, Maybelle, and Giff exclaim in dismay.

'What's the matter?' Jessie whispered.

'There's a snairie nest ahead,' Maybelle muttered in her ear. 'See that big round thing hanging in the tree? By the look of it, the snairies aren't at home, so we'd better be careful. They like hiding under dead leaves, you know, the silly things.'

'Snairies?' hissed Jessie, her eyes still fixed on the tip of the Rainbow Wand. 'What are—?'

And at that very moment, she trod on something round and bouncy. The thing squeaked loudly, and Jessie jumped backward with a cry of shock.

A small, round creature erupted from the forest floor in a shower of dead leaves, squeaking indignantly. The creature's body was not much bigger than a tennis ball. It had big blue eyes and very large bright pink feet. Otherwise, it was completely covered in long, silky brown hair.

'Oh, I'm really sorry!' Jessie exclaimed. 'I didn't mean to tread on you.'

Still squeaking, the little creature began bouncing up and down like a hairy ball with feet. Then, suddenly, the forest floor was dotted with what looked like tiny explosions of dead leaves. Other snairies were popping up everywhere, their blue eyes wide and startled.

Jessie took another step backward. 'Will they hurt us?' she whispered.

'Of course not,' snorted Maybelle, pawing the ground. 'They'll only waste our time. Snairies are very good at that, and they enjoy it, too.'

'Well, they haven't got anything else to do, have they?' Patrice said distractedly. 'Has anyone got any peppermints?'

'I've got two,' Giff squeaked. 'I was saving them for—'

'Give them to me, Giff,' ordered Patrice, holding out her hand.

'But I was saving them for—' Giff began.

'Give her the peppermints!' shouted Maybelle. 'This is an emergency!'

Sulkily, Giff took two rather worn-looking peppermints from under his cap, and gave them to Patrice. Patrice put them onto the palm of her hand and held them out to the snairie Jessie had trodden on.

'Treats!' she cooed, in a sing-song voice. 'Treats, to say sorry for the hurt.'

The snairie glanced around at its friends. 'Treats,' it said longingly.

'A riddle!' chorused the other snairies, bouncing up and down and slapping the dead leaves with their big pink feet. 'A riddle, *then* treats, when we get the answer!'

'Oh, no,' Giff groaned.

Maybelle frowned, lashing her tail furiously. 'Listen, snairies!' she snapped. 'We're on important business. We haven't got time to stand around asking you riddles!'

The snairies looked at one another. Then, as if obeying some secret signal, they all dived back under the leaves. The leaves heaved and rustled, then grew silent, but Jessie could feel several small, round bodies pressing against the toes of her shoes.

'Look what you've done, Maybelle!' Patrice said crossly. 'Now they'll keep rolling under our feet so we tread on them with every step we take. You know how they are.'

'Well, let's just tread on them, then,' bellowed Maybelle, in a temper. 'I don't care if every one of the stupid, useless things is squashed flat!'

'Oh, don't say that!' cried Jessie in distress. 'We mustn't hurt them!'

Patrice sighed. 'We'll have to ask them a riddle,' she said. 'It's the only way.'

'I know lots of riddles,' Jessie said eagerly. 'What about—?'

'Be careful, Jessie!' Giff whimpered, shuffling his feet nervously. 'They're listening!'

'It has to be a really, really easy riddle, dearie,' Patrice explained in a low voice as Jessie glanced at Giff in surprise. 'If the snairies can't think of an answer, they'll get upset.'

'Then they'll roll under our feet even more,' moaned Giff. 'We'll be stuck here for ages. That happened to my mother once.'

'What did she ask them?' Jessie whispered.

'She couldn't think of anything,' Giff whispered back. 'So the snairies all crowded around her feet and wouldn't move. She didn't want to tread on them, so she had to sleep the night in the forest, standing up!'

Maybelle snorted in disgust.

'Jessie!' hissed Patrice. 'Look at the wand!'

Jessie felt a thrill of fear as she saw that the golden tip of the Rainbow Wand was fading to yellow. She thought frantically.

'Give me the peppermints, Patrice,' she said at last. When she had the peppermints in her hand she held them out and cleared her throat. 'All right, snairies!' she called. 'Here's a riddle for you!'

Dead leaves flew into the air as the snairies popped their heads up again. 'Now, listen carefully,' Jessie said. 'What has a name beginning with "s", has two blue eyes and two pink feet, is covered in brown hair, has a round nest, hides under dead leaves and loves to answer riddles?'

The snairies stood motionless, thinking hard.

'Not a brain in their heads,' muttered Maybelle, ignoring Patrice's frantic shushing sounds.

The snairies began whispering together. They seemed to be having an argument.

'How could they *possibly* not know the answer?' Jessie whispered in despair.

'You don't know snairies,' Maybelle said darkly.

But just then, the snairie Jessie had trodden on looked up. 'Is . . . is the answer, "a snairie"?' it said hesitantly.

'Yes!' Jessie exclaimed.

All the snairies began bouncing up and down. 'We were right! We were right!' they squeaked together. 'Treats!' And without any warning, they all leaped wildly at the peppermints in Jessie's outstretched hand.

Taken by surprise, Jessie staggered backward, losing her balance. The Rainbow Wand twisted in her hand. The snairies crashed into it headlong. There was a blinding flash, and a sharp, cracking sound.

Jessie screamed in fright. For a moment she could see nothing but stars, and when at last her eyes cleared, the forest floor was deserted. The snairies had completely disappeared. 'Oh, no!' she cried in horror.

'It's all right!' Giff squealed. 'Look!' He pointed at the snairie nest, which was now studded all over with pairs of bright pink feet, as if the snairies had dived in headfirst.

'The wand sent them home!' exclaimed Patrice. 'Oh, quickly, let's get out of here before they come out again!'

CHAPTER EIGHT

The Lost One

s Jessie led the way past the snairie nest, one of the pairs of feet disappeared inside, and a hairy face with two bright blue eyes peeped out. Jessie thought she recognised the snairie she'd trodden on, and her stomach lurched.

'Hello,' mumbled the snairie. 'Who are you?'

'Oh, no-one special,' Patrice said quickly. 'Don't let us disturb you.'

The snairie nodded sleepily. It ducked back into the nest again, and the next moment the four friends were staring at the soles of its feet once more, and gentle snores were filling the air.

'They've forgotten us already!' called Jessie as she

and the others ran on. 'Do you think the Rainbow Wand made them lose their memories?'

'It might have,' Patrice puffed. 'It must have given them an awful shock when it flashed and blew them home like that. Lucky it was only yellow at the time. Otherwise—'

She broke off as Jessie gave a joyous cry and held the wand high. The tip was rapidly brightening, changing from yellow to gold to orange. 'Tasha must be very near!' Jessie shouted. 'Come on!'

The Rainbow Wand led Jessie, Patrice, Maybelle, and Giff out of the grove of pale-leafed trees, and into a thick mass of berry bushes. It was shining more brightly every moment, but there was still no sign of Tasha.

'Where are we?' Jessie shouted over her shoulder.

There was no answer. Surprised, she slowed down and looked back. All her friends were smiling.

'We should have known,' Maybelle said gruffly.

'Of *course!*' Patrice sighed.

'They miss Queen Helena,' Giff said. 'You can't really blame them.'

'What are you talking about?' Jessie demanded. 'What do you—?'

Then she pushed through the last of the berry

bushes. And, dazzled by the flaming red light of the Rainbow Wand, she blinked at what was ahead.

It was a field of giant flowers—flowers of every kind, some as tall as small trees, bending and swaying in the soft Realm breeze.

Filled with wonder, Jessie moved forward. Rich brown earth crumbled beneath her feet. Slender green stems and leaves swayed all around her. Soft colours blended above her head. Sweet perfumes scented the air, which was filled with soft, faint music as if the flowers themselves were singing.

The Rainbow Wand was brightening every moment. Jessie told herself she should be calling Tasha's name, but somehow she couldn't bear to break into the sound of the flowers' song. Then she saw a small green space ahead—a round clearing in the middle of the flower field. Jessie began to move faster, but as she reached the clearing's edge, she stopped, staring.

A little blue rabbit was joyfully hopping around the clearing, pausing now and then to nibble the soft green grass. High above the rabbit's head, dancing in a ring with glorious flowers nodding all around them were Daisy, Violet, Daffodil, Bluebell, and Rose. And in the middle of their circle, eyes sparkling, silver wings fluttering and alive, danced Tasha.

'Jessie!' squeaked Daffodil, seeing Jessie and turning an excited somersault in the air. 'You've come back after all! Oh, what a beautiful wand! See how brightly it shines!'

The Rainbow Wand was blazing. Its tip was a glittering scarlet star. Tasha looked down, and her eyes widened.

'Did you fairies bring this little girl into the Realm?' said Patrice sternly. 'How could you! You *know* it's against the rules.'

'We didn't bring her!' cried Daffodil indignantly. 'She came in all by herself!'

Tasha nodded proudly. 'I went into your special garden and I said, "Open," and my hair blew around,' she said to Jessie. 'And then I was in fairyland.'

'We met Tasha on the pebbly road,' Rose broke in, holding out her full pink skirts and twirling around. 'She was all alone except for Bunny. And when we asked her if she'd dance with us, she said yes! She said she'd *love* to dance with us. And she had her own wings, and everything.'

'So we brought her to the Forest of Flowers with us,' Violet put in shyly.

'That was a good idea, Jessie, wasn't it?' shouted Daffodil. 'Because Tasha likes flowers. And Bunny likes them, too.'

Tasha's face was shining. Jessie couldn't bring herself to do anything more than smile and nod.

'It was a lovely idea,' she said gently. 'But Tasha shouldn't have left Blue Moon without asking her mother. We've been very worried, and we've been looking for her everywhere. Anyway, now it's time for her to come home.'

'Oh, no!' wailed the fairies. 'Not yet!'

Jessie had expected Tasha to argue, too, but the little girl just nodded sadly. 'I have to go now,' she told the flower fairies. 'Jessie says.'

Silver wings fluttering, she let herself drift slowly to the ground. 'Come on, Bunny,' she said. The little blue rabbit jumped into her arms, and she began skipping toward Jessie through the flowers.

'Don't come too near the wand, fairies,' Jessie warned as the fairies began to follow. 'It might hurt you.'

She saw how disappointed they looked and thought quickly. 'Can you fly in front of us, though?' she added. 'Can you lead us back to the Door by the quickest way?'

'I know the quickest way,' said Maybelle. 'Why in the Realm—?' Patrice nudged her sharply and she fell silent.

Very pleased to have an important job to do,

Daisy, Buttercup, Rose, Violet, and Bluebell flew over to a stem of pink-spotted bells, and perched there, waiting.

Tasha reached Jessie's side and took her hand. Jessie's whole arm tingled, and the Rainbow Wand flamed like a fiery star.

'That thing's looking dangerous,' Maybelle muttered nervously. 'Say the words to break the spell, Jessie.'

'Not till Tasha's safely home,' Jessie said. 'I'm not taking any risks.' She smiled at Tasha. 'Look what I found,' she said, digging into her pocket and bringing out the butterfly hair clip. Tasha beamed as the butterfly was clipped to her hair once more.

'This way!' squeaked Daffodil, beckoning importantly. 'This way!'

Following the fairies, Jessie began to lead Tasha through the flowers, with Patrice, Giff and Maybelle following in single file behind.

'Are you a fairy princess, Jessie?' Tasha asked breathlessly.

'She certainly is, dearie,' said Patrice warmly, just as Jessie was about to deny that she was any such thing.

'I knew she was,' said Tasha. 'She has a fairy princess wand.' She yawned and cuddled Bunny closer to her chest. She was clearly very sleepy, but she trotted beside Jessie without complaint as the fairies led them out of the Forest of Flowers, through a group of trees with silver bark, and on to the pebbly road.

When at last the Door came into view, even Jessie was feeling tired. It seemed to her that she'd been in the Realm for ages, though the sun was still high in the sky, so she knew it hadn't been so very long at all.

'With a bit of luck, Mrs Tweedie will still be out searching the streets,' she whispered to Patrice, Maybelle, and Giff. 'I might be able to get Tasha into the house before she gets back.'

'The Tweedie woman won't be satisfied with that,' Maybelle muttered. 'She'll want to know where the child has been. She'll ask her all sorts of questions.'

'I've thought of that,' Jessie said. 'If I can get Tasha back to the house, I'll put her on my bed to lie down. She's really tired—I'm sure she'll go straight to sleep. Then I'll tell Mrs Tweedie she was there all the time.'

'You might get away with it,' Patrice said doubtfully. 'We'll keep our fingers crossed.'

'And our toes,' said Giff.

The flower fairies hovered in front of the Door, their wings bright in the sunlight. 'We'll come with you, Jessie,' said Daffodil brightly. 'Then we can look for sweetie-pies again.'

'If greedy Emerald hasn't found them all,' said Rose, licking her lips.

'No, no,' Jessie said firmly. 'Tasha and I have to go alone this time. You stay where you are. And if Emerald's in the secret garden, I'll send her home, too.'

Holding the Rainbow Wand carefully to one side, she bent and picked Tasha up. 'Hold tight, Tasha,' she said softly.

The little girl waved to the fairies, Patrice, Maybelle, and Giff. Then she put her arm around Jessie's neck. Jessie turned and faced the door.

'Open!' she said. Everything grew dark. Her hair began to blow around her head. The cool wind tingled on her face. She could faintly hear the sounds of her friends calling goodbye and wishing her luck. She could feel Tasha clinging to her.

And then there was grass beneath her feet, and she could hear Flynn yowling somewhere nearby. Her arm was aching with Tasha's weight. She opened her eyes, and at once they began to water in the sunlight. Sighing with relief, she dropped the

Rainbow Wand, then bent and let Tasha slide to the ground.

'We're back, Bunny,' she heard the little girl yawn. 'We're back from the Realm.'

'So you are, you clever girl!' cooed a fake-sweet voice. 'And now you can tell me all about it, can't you?'

Jessie jerked upright, spun around, and found herself looking straight into the cold, triumphant eyes of Mrs Tweedie.

CHAPTER NINE

The Trap

'Don't bother trying to make up a story to explain this, Jessie,' said Mrs Tweedie as Jessie gaped at her, speechless with shock. 'I saw Tasha disappear through the Door, I saw you go after her, and just now I saw you both come back. I saw it with my own eyes—just as I'd planned.'

She waited, a smile curving her thin lips, while slowly Jessie made sense of what she'd said, and Flynn yowled on the other side of the door in the hedge.

'You knew where Tasha was all the time,' Jessie whispered. 'That note you left for me was a lie. You sent Tasha to the Realm, and then you tricked me into going after her.'

'Quite. And I watched it all from the top of a ladder on the other side of the hedge,' Mrs Tweedie said, her smile broadening. 'You didn't notice me— even that cat didn't see me till I came down. Then it attacked me, the vicious brute!'

She looked down at her hands, which were covered in deep scarlet scratches, then glanced at the door in the hedge, as if to make sure that Flynn was still safely locked outside.

'I admit I was very annoyed when you insisted on staying home today, Jessie,' she went on. 'I'd gone to a lot of trouble to get Blue Moon to myself, and arrange to babysit Tasha on the same day. Then I realised that you could make my plan even better. So I set my little trap, and you fell into it.'

Jessie wet her lips. 'No-one will believe you, if you tell,' she said. 'They'll say you were seeing things.'

'I'm not Mr Bins, Jessie,' said Mrs Tweedie softly. 'I'm famous for investigating mysteries like this. Well, you should know. You're reading one of my books, after all.'

She raised an eyebrow, waiting for Jessie to realise what she meant. And slowly, with cold, prickling horror, Jessie did.

'You're L.T. Bowers,' Jessie gasped.

'That's right,' the woman said, her voice

hardening. 'Louise Tweedie Bowers. When the Bins family moved into my block of flats, it was the stroke of luck I'd been waiting for all my writing life. I'd always been interested in Robert Belairs. Those fairy paintings of his are so detailed—so *real*! Then I heard what the Bins family had to say, and the rest is history—or will be.'

She pointed to a place near the top of the hedge. Something glinted there—the lens of her video camera, wedged between dense leaves.

'Everything that has happened here today has been recorded,' she said, eyeing Jessie's shocked face with satisfaction. 'And I've taken hundreds of still photographs over the past few months, too, of course. My readers like pictures.'

Jessie felt sick. 'You planned it all,' she said in a low voice. 'You came here to spy on us. You—'

'I've also got sound recordings,' Mrs Tweedie cut in. 'Lately I've had plenty of chances to plant a recording device in here for a day or two. That's how I knew to tell Tasha that the magic word was "Open."'

Jessie looked quickly over her shoulder. Tasha had curled up on the grass and gone peacefully to sleep with her blue rabbit in her arms. Beside her lay the butterfly hair clip, which had again fallen from her tangled curls.

'Sweet!' purred Mrs Tweedie. 'Oh, she'll be wonderful on television.'

'You can't write about this, Mrs Tweedie,' Jessie said, trying to control the trembling in her voice. 'You'll destroy Blue Moon. You'll threaten the Realm itself. You can't—'

Mrs Tweedie laughed. 'If you think that I left my lovely, convenient flat and camped for months in that dreadful house next door for fun, you're wrong,' she said. 'Today is my last day here, and I couldn't be happier. I've already returned the car to the hire company, and sent all my things back to the city—well, except for the evidence, of course. I wouldn't let that out of my sight.' She patted the little overnight bag at her feet and sighed with pleasure.

'This will be the biggest story of my life,' she went on smugly. 'After the first few newspaper stories and TV interviews, publishers will be wild to get the book. I'll be able to name my own price. Oh, the timing is perfect! People who'd never heard of Robert Belairs or Blue Moon know all about them now, because of the exhibition.'

She glanced at her watch. 'Actually, some people from one of the TV stations should be here any minute,' she added casually. 'A news story tonight will get the ball rolling.'

Jessie clenched her fists. 'I'll tell them that nothing you say is true,' she said in a low voice. 'I'll tell them that you faked the video, and the pictures, and everything.'

'Say what you like,' drawled Mrs Tweedie. 'Tasha is a very truthful little girl. *She* won't tell fibs. It was a very good idea to use her for my little experiment.'

'You only used Tasha because you couldn't get into the Realm yourself,' Jessie burst out. 'You probably tried over and over again, but you couldn't do it. I suppose you think it's because you're a grown-up, but it's not! It's because you're mean and selfish and horrible, and the Realm won't have you!'

Anger flashed in Mrs Tweedie's eyes. 'Thank you for that information,' she sneered. 'And now, here's something for you to think about!'

She turned around, felt under a rosemary bush, and pulled out a small green cage. Jessie went cold as she saw, crouching behind the narrow bars, a tiny, terrified figure with soft green wings—the rainbow fairy Emerald.

Jessie jumped forward, but Mrs Tweedie swung the cage out of her reach. There was a rattling sound and a tiny striped sweet rolled through the bars and fell onto the grass.

In a flash, Jessie saw what she should have realised long ago. It was Mrs Tweedie who had been leaving treats for the fairies in the secret garden. She'd been doing it for weeks—ever since Granny went away. And this morning she'd laid her trap, knowing that she was sure to catch at least one fairy by the end of the day.

'I don't think there'll be any risk of people thinking I'm a fake when they see this, do you?' Mrs Tweedie said softly.

'Hello?' a crisp female voice called from behind the door in the hedge. 'Ms Bowers?'

'Ye-es!' carolled Mrs Tweedie, pushing Jessie away and returning the cage to its hiding place.

The door opened and Flynn streaked in, nearly tripping up the smartly dressed young woman and the tall, bearded man standing outside. Mrs Tweedie shrank back in alarm, but Flynn just leaped under a rosemary bush and crouched there in sullen silence.

'Ms Bowers? I'm Sharon Bliss. We spoke on the phone,' the young woman said, moving forward and holding out her hand to Mrs Tweedie.

'Good to meet you,' said Mrs Tweedie, shaking hands. She smiled at the bearded man, who was carrying a camcorder.

'Kel Pike,' he said with a casual nod. He lifted the camera onto his shoulder. 'Where's this fairy, then?' he asked. He sounded as if he was trying not to laugh. Sharon glanced at him warningly.

'Louise, have you lost your mind?' snapped a voice.

Everyone jumped and turned. Ms Stone was standing in the doorway, her face rigid with anger. 'I was outside in my car, waiting to speak to Jessica's mother when she got home, when these people arrived,' she said icily. 'They told me—they told me that they'd come to interview a woman who claimed to have caught a—a *fairy*.'

'That's right,' said Mrs Tweedie calmly.

'Louise!' Ms Stone snapped. 'It's bad enough making a fool of yourself, but how *could* you drag Jessica into this? The child's damaged enough as it is. That grandmother of hers—' She broke off and swung around to Sharon Bliss. 'This is just a stupid publicity stunt for the Belairs exhibition, can't you see that?' she exclaimed. 'How *can* you go along with it?'

Sharon shrugged. 'People like fun stories like this on a Sunday night,' she said. 'The boss says that L.T. Bowers is always good for a laugh.'

'L.T. Bowers?' hissed Ms Stone, staring at her. 'But—'

'I think it's time to put an end to all this,' Mrs Tweedie said coldly. She lifted the cage from behind her, and held it up with a small, triumphant smile.

Everyone stared. Gauzy wings glimmered behind bars as the cage swung in Mrs Tweedie's hand.

There was a short, deadly silence.

'We can't do anything with this, Sharon,' said Kel Pike at last. 'No way. She didn't even try to give it a face, or legs, or anything.'

Mrs Tweedie looked into the cage, and her eyes bulged. The cage tilted, the door swung open, and Tasha's butterfly hair clip slid out and dropped softly to the ground.

Tears of relief welled up in Jessie's eyes. She clapped her hands over her mouth to hold back hysterical laughter. She heard a soft trill behind her and swung around. Flynn was sitting there, calmly washing his paws, to which fragments of earth still clung. He met her eyes and blinked.

Mrs Tweedie pointed at him, beside herself with rage. 'It was that cat!' she shrieked. 'The cat crept around behind the bushes! He let the fairy out, and put this thing in its place!' She kicked at the butterfly hair clip, and missed.

'The cat,' drawled Kel Pike. 'Sure.' He looked at Sharon Bliss, and jerked his head toward the door.

'Yes. Well. We'll be off, then,' Sharon said in a high voice. 'Thanks very much.'

The two of them almost ran through the door and out into the garden beyond. With a final, appalled glance at Mrs Tweedie, Ms Stone stalked after them, obviously intending to make sure they actually left.

'Stop grinning, you stupid girl!' Mrs Tweedie snarled at Jessie. 'This doesn't make a scrap of difference! I still have the pictures and the tapes. The whole world's going to know about you and this place. I said, *get that smile off your face!*'

Wild with fury, she hurled the empty cage at Jessie. Flynn sprang at her like an orange fury.

'Get away from me, you brute!' the woman shrieked. She tore the biting, scratching cat away from her and threw him aside. Flynn landed lightly and spun around, ready to attack again.

Mrs Tweedie looked around for a weapon. Her eyes fell on the Rainbow Wand, lying on the grass where Jessie had dropped it. Teeth bared, she leaped for it.

'No!' Jessie screamed. 'No—'

Mrs Tweedie grabbed the wand with both hands. Instantly it was as if the secret garden had been struck by scarlet lightning. There was an ear-splitting crack . . .

And when Jessie was able to look again, the grass was littered with charred fragments of leather and melted plastic, Flynn was peacefully washing his paws once more, and Mrs Tweedie had gone.

CHAPTER TEN

Surprises

rembling with shock, Jessie crawled to the Rainbow Wand and took it in her hand. 'The Lost One is found,' she mumbled. At once the wand faded, becoming a plain silver rod once more.

'Something went bang, Jessie.'

Jessie turned around. Tasha was sitting up, rubbing her eyes. 'Never mind,' Jessie said hurriedly. She picked up the butterfly hair clip from the grass, and took it to the little girl. 'You lost this again,' she said, clipping the butterfly to the dark curls.

'Well, hello, you two,' said a bright voice from the door.

'Mummy!' squealed Tasha. She scrambled up and

ran to the smiling woman, who crouched to hug her.

'You must be Jessie,' the woman said, smiling at Jessie over her daughter's head. 'I'm Alice, Tasha's mum. Thank you so much for looking after her today. Where's Mrs Tweedie?'

'I'm—I'm not sure,' Jessie stammered, getting unsteadily to her feet. 'She . . . um . . . went somewhere.'

'Oh,' Alice said. 'Well, could you thank her very much for me? I'd like to get Tasha home. I think a storm might be coming. I heard thunder a moment ago.' She stood up, with Tasha in her arms. 'Home we go, sweetie,' she said as Tasha snuggled into her shoulder. 'Oh, you're a tired girl, aren't you?'

Tasha nodded sleepily. 'I went to sleep on the grass,' she said. 'Mum? I went to fairyland. I danced with flower fairies. And I met an elf, and a little white horse that talked. And Jessie was a fairy princess with a magic wand.'

'Is that so?' her mother said, glancing at Jessie with a puzzled smile. Jessie held her breath.

'Yes,' Tasha said. 'And Mum? Bunny came alive.' She sighed happily, and yawned. 'I like sleeping on grass,' she added, closing her eyes. 'That was the bestest dream I ever had.'

Alice kissed the top of her head, waved good-bye to Jessie, and hurried away through the trees. Flynn went with her, but Jessie stayed at the doorway of the secret garden. Her legs were trembling so much that she wasn't sure they would carry her. She stood motionless, staring at nothing.

Tasha thought that the Realm had been a dream, a wonderful dream. Jessie felt as if she were living in a dream right now. Her mind was numb. Blue Moon was safe. The Realm was safe. But . . . Mrs Tweedie. What had the Rainbow Wand done to Mrs Tweedie?

Suddenly she realised that something was moving among the trees. She blinked, and as her eyes came back into focus her heart leaped. Her grandmother was hurrying toward the secret garden, still dressed in the blue skirt and loose, flowered jacket she wore for travelling. Flynn was trotting by Granny's side, his tail held high.

Neither of them seemed to be aware that Ms Stone was following them. Jessie groaned aloud. Oh, why won't Stoneface leave me alone? she thought desperately. I've got to talk to Granny by herself. I've just got to!

'Jessie, are you all right?' Granny exclaimed, reaching Jessie and hugging her tightly. 'When

Flynn told me I . . . oh, Jessie, I can't believe I left you to face this alone! I'm so sorry!'

'I should think so!' snapped Ms Stone, striding up behind her, breathing hard. 'You should be ashamed of yourself, Mrs Belairs—involving your granddaughter in a crude publicity stunt. And as for that poor, silly Louise Tweedie—'

Granny turned around. 'I don't think we've met,' she said mildly, looking up into Ms Stone's frozen face. Then she stiffened. 'Oh, you poor child,' she murmured, in quite a different voice. And to Jessie's astonishment, she reached out and took Ms Stone's hands in both her own.

Ugly patches of crimson appeared on Ms Stone's cheeks and neck. A strange, almost frightened, expression sprang into her eyes. 'Let me go!' she gasped, trying to wrench her hands free.

Granny held on. It was as if, suddenly, she had twice her usual strength. Jessie's skin prickled. 'Granny,' she whispered urgently. 'It's Ms Stone— you know—my school teacher!'

Granny didn't answer. Her eyes were fixed on Ms Stone's. 'Don't be afraid, my dear,' she said softly, backing through the secret garden doorway and pulling the terrified-looking woman with her. 'All will be well. Come with me, now. Come on.'

Amazed and fearful, Jessie stumbled out of the way as slowly but surely her grandmother drew Ms Stone into the centre of the secret garden.

And, without warning, the Rainbow Wand blazed with radiant light. Jessie screamed as sparks flew from the burning star at its tip, showering the soft green grass, the fragrant rosemary, like scarlet rain.

What could this mean? Why was the wand acting as if . . . as if . . . ?

It is tuned to find Linnet, and always will be, while I live . . .

'It can't be!' Jessie whispered, as Avron's voice echoed in her mind. She turned and stared at Ms Stone, who was cowering away from the blinding glare. She felt her grandmother push Ms Stone's hand into hers. 'Open!' Granny called in a thunderous voice.

Jessie's hair began to fly around her head. Ms Stone whimpered beside her. As darkness closed in, her grandmother's voice rang in her ears.

'Lyn Stone is a Lost One, Jessie!' Granny called. 'That wand knows it—and I knew it the minute I set eyes on her! Don't you see? That's why she's hated magic for so long. It's in her blood! It made her a stranger in this world, but she didn't know why, so she's been afraid of it for most of her life.

Take her home, Jessie! Take the poor child home!'

An hour later, Jessie came back to Blue Moon. She found her mother and grandmother in the kitchen, drinking tea and eating pastries they'd bought on their way home from the airport.

'I'm so glad you decided to go out after all, Jess,' Rosemary said, when the greetings were over and Jessie had joined them at the table. 'Really, you were quite right about Louise Tweedie. She's a very peculiar woman. Do you know, she's just packed up and left?'

'Really?' Jessie said weakly.

'Yes!' Rosemary exclaimed. 'And, what's more, she seems to have been burning rubbish in the garden. There are little bits of melted plastic and metal and paper all over the grass. I'll really give her a piece of my mind when she turns up again!'

Jessie sank her teeth into an apricot pastry. 'I don't think she will,' she said with her mouth full. 'I think she's gone home—back where she came from—and that she's forgotten all about us.'

Rosemary laughed. 'I wish!' she said.

Jessie smiled. She knew she was right. After all, as Patrice had reminded her just half an hour ago, that's what had happened to the snairies when *they* touched the Rainbow Wand.

'Oh,' said Granny, stretching out her legs, comfortable in old slacks once more. 'It's wonderful to be back at Blue Moon.'

'It certainly is,' Rosemary agreed. 'One day in the city was enough for me.' She took a deep breath and looked at Jessie, who had just taken another big bite of her pastry.

'Today I spoke to our lawyer, and also to the estate agent who manages the renting of our old house, Jess,' she said. 'The young couple who rent the house have wanted to buy it for ages, you know. They're offering a good price, they're nice people, and I'm tired of having all that money tied up in a house we'll never live in again. So finally I've told the agent that, yes, we'll sell. Why not? Our home is here now.'

Jessie nearly choked on her pastry. 'Mum!' she spluttered. 'You mean . . . *that's* why you went to the city so early?'

'Well, yes,' said Rosemary, smiling. 'I didn't tell you before because I wanted to make sure it was really going to happen.'

'Well, this *is* exciting!' Granny said, her eyes twinkling. 'What made you decide at last, my darling?'

Rosemary shrugged. 'Oh—I don't know,' she said, not looking at Jessie. 'Yesterday, I talked to someone who—who was obviously very bitter, and very unhappy, but still wanted everyone else to live their lives the way she did. I was very sad for her. She didn't seem to understand how important it is to love what you do—whatever it is, and whatever form it takes.'

She put down her cup and sighed. 'Talking to her made me realise that you should treasure happiness and trust it,' she said. 'And home—well, home is where the heart is, as they say.' She wiped a trace of dampness from her eyes and laughed self-consciously.

Jessie flung her arms around her mother's neck and hugged her. Her mind was full of pictures. She remembered Ms Stone—Linnet of the Realm now—her shining hair streaming down her back, her eyes glowing, her face alive with happiness. She thought of stern Avron weeping with joy because his child had been found. She thought of Patrice, Giff, Maybelle, and all the Folk celebrating the return of their Lost One, and the golden palace ringing with their songs of joy.

'You're so right, Mum!' she said. 'You're so really, really right!'

Rosemary laughed again. 'I knew you'd be pleased,' she said. Then she looked carefully at the charm bracelet on Jessie's wrist. 'Oh, Jessie, you've got a new charm!' she exclaimed. 'A little gold crown. Isn't that sweet? Where did it come from?'

'Jessie earned it, I'd say,' Granny said, beaming. 'I'd say that someone decided that every true, brave princess should have a crown to call her own. Isn't that so, Jessie?'

And Jessie, thinking of Avron's words as he fastened the tiny crown in place, blushed, and nodded.

'May you always feel for others, as you do now,' Avron had said, with a deep bow. 'May you always remember the importance of laughter. And may there always be magic in your heart. Then, Princess Jessie of the Realm, you will indeed live happily ever after.'

IF YOU'VE ENJOYED THE STORIES IN THIS BOOK, LOOK OUT

FOR ANOTHER BOOK IN THE FAIRY CHARM SERIES. HERE

IS A SHORT EXTRACT FROM *THE WATER SPRITES*.

An Invitation

essie fastened her charm bracelet around her wrist and checked her reflection in the mirror. Her green eyes were sparkling. Her golden red hair shone against the rich blue of her new dress. She looked happy and excited, and no wonder! It was a sunny Saturday afternoon, and she was going to a party. Not an ordinary party, either, but a party in the magical world of the Realm.

The charm bracelet jingled softly as Jessie picked up the gold-speckled leaf lying beside her hairbrush. When she'd found the leaf on her desk a couple of days before, she'd thought at first that it was quite ordinary. She thought the breeze had blown it through her open window.

She'd never seen a leaf just like it before, but that wasn't surprising. The garden of Blue Moon, her grandmother's old house in the mountains, was filled with unusual trees and bushes. Though she and her mother had been living with Granny for over a year, Jessie was still discovering plants that were new to her.

But when she picked up the speckled leaf, she suddenly saw that there was something strange about it. The yellow speckles were in straight lines, set tidily one above the other. Jessie peered at them closely. And then she realised that the speckles were words! The leaf was covered in tiny yellow writing.

Jessie smiled as she remembered how astonished and delighted she'd been as she read the leaf's message for the first time.

Princess Jessie! The village of Lirralee invites you to baby Jewel's Welcome Party on Saturday afternoon. The party begins at three o'clock and ends when the birds go to bed. There will be music, dancing, games, and lots of food. Please come!

On the other side of the leaf there was another message, in different handwriting.

Hope you can come, Jessie. Giff and Maybelle are invited, too. Be at my place at 2:30 and we can all go together. Lirralee is my old home village. Everyone is longing to meet you. Love, Patrice.

Jessie had been very relieved to read that note. She had no idea where Lirralee was, but with her friends Patrice the palace housekeeper, Giff the elf, and Maybelle the miniature horse to guide her, she wouldn't get lost.

She glanced at the clock on her bedside table and was startled to see that it was after two o'clock. Time had flown. If she didn't hurry, she'd be late. She grabbed the gift she'd wrapped in silver paper, and hurried out of her room to find her grandmother.

Voices were floating from the kitchen. Jessie sighed as she recognised the chirping tones of Mrs Tweedie, the next-door neighbour.

What a nuisance! Mrs Tweedie was a very curious woman. If she saw Jessie heading for the bottom of the Blue Moon garden dressed in party clothes, she'd ask all sorts of questions.

Jessie hesitated, wondering if she should just slip out of the front door without saying goodbye. Her mother was out for the day, and Granny would understand.

'I'm so upset!' Mrs Tweedie wailed. 'I was terribly fond of that ring. It was my mother's.'

'I'm sure you'll find it, Louise,' Granny said soothingly. 'It's probably just fallen—'

'No!' Mrs Tweedie insisted. 'It was on my bedside table, in a little crystal dish. I remember *perfectly*. I put it there before I did the washing. I *always* put it there. That Wiseman person who came to clean the windows took it. I *know* he did.'

Jessie's eyes widened, and she felt heat rush into her face. Mr Wiseman was the father of her friend Sal. He was a kind, cheerful man, always full of jokes and fun, just like Sal. What was Mrs Tweedie saying about him?

She rushed into the kitchen. Granny and Mrs Tweedie turned to look at her.

'Is that a new outfit, dear?' asked Mrs Tweedie, her sharp little nose twitching as she looked Jessie up and down. 'I don't think I've seen it before. It's very pretty. Are you going to a party?'

'Yes,' Jessie said breathlessly. 'But, Mrs Tweedie, I couldn't help hearing what you were saying about

Mr Wiseman just now, and—'

Mrs Tweedie's face grew solemn. 'It's not very nice, I know,' she said. 'I hate to accuse anyone, but facts are facts. I can't go to the police—I mean, the man will just deny he took my ring, won't he? But I know he did it, and it's only right to warn people about him.'

'Louise, believe me, Alf Wiseman is no thief!' Granny said very firmly. 'He's been in and out of Blue Moon for years—ever since he started his window-cleaning business. He's as honest as the day is long.'

'Of course he is!' Jessie exclaimed. 'He's my friend's dad. I know him really well.'

Mrs Tweedie looked at her sorrowfully. 'I *am* sorry, dear,' she said. 'But, sadly, people aren't always what they seem.'

'Jessie, you'd better go, or you'll be late,' Granny said, as Jessie opened her mouth to argue. 'You'll have to run as it is.'

'Don't tell me you're *walking* to the party, dear?' cried Mrs Tweedie as Jessie hurried to the door. 'In your nice dress and shoes? No, no. Come on, I'll drive you.'

'No!' Jessie exclaimed, horrified. 'I mean, thank you, but it isn't far. I don't need a lift.'

'It's no trouble!' said Mrs Tweedie. 'I must go, anyway. I just popped in for a minute to see if your grandmother wanted anything at the supermarket.'

And to spread rumours about Mr Wiseman, Jessie thought furiously. But the anger was driven from her mind as Mrs Tweedie picked up her handbag and car keys from the kitchen table and bustled to join her at the door.

'Now, where's this party? Which street?' Mrs Tweedie asked brightly.